Delin

Praise for *Confessi*

There are parts of *Confessions of a Not-So-Average Girl* that would be hard to believe, if you didn't know the author was telling her own story. Donna addresses some of the most difficult problems of sociology and theology with a simplicity and grace that reminds the reader of both the incredible resiliency of any given individual, and God's great commitment to redeem anything anyone—absolutely anything, and absolutely anyone—is willing to truly give over to him.

For youth who are facing the all-too-common struggles Donna experienced, this book will be a comfort and a guide. For those who are being raised in families where security and privilege are taken for granted, Donna's account could prompt awareness of and empathy for those of their peers who, Scripture says, are the blessed—"the poor in spirit."

GREG PAUL

Author of *God in the Alley: Being and Seeing Jesus in a Broken World*, and *The Twenty Piece Shuffle: Why the Poor and the Rich Need Each Other*. Founder of Sanctuary Ministries of Toronto

—

Wow, what a book! I read the manuscript on a flight to Los Angeles and wept the whole flight. Donna is thoroughly versed in what is happening in the world of adolescence. Her own story of painful life experiences, sprinkled with the hope of Christ and eventually the overall healing of Jesus, is powerfully told on each page of this wonderful and useful book. Youth Workers, pastors and especially teenage girls who face the broken world of adolescent pain will find this book very helpful in bringing the hope that only Jesus can provide. I know I will use this book in our ministry to families in the government housing neighbourhoods we serve. Thank you, Donna, for your heartbreaking honesty. This book will make a difference in so many lives.

REVEREND COLIN MCCARTNEY
Founding Director, UrbanPromise, Toronto, Ontario

—

Confessions plunges head-first into the heartache of a young girl drowning in familial brokenness. Armed with only her life-preserver journal, young Donna, with blunt, colourful simplicity, explores the fragments of her adolescent heart placing them firmly in the hands of her best friend, Jesus. This is a spirited book of hope for kids... including the adult kind.

JASON HILDEBRAND
Actor, creative catalyst and award-winning filmmaker of
The Prodigal Trilogy

—

Have you ever found yourself teaching and wondering what the life story is of the child before you? Donna writes with clarity, vivid recall, and pain, interspersed with humour, the story of growing up in a broken home. It is her story, but I am certain way too many children in our midst identify with much of it. Once you have read *Confessions*, you will want every child you teach to also read it, for Donna story will help children who feel "*not-so-average*" feel like they are not-so-alone. As a diary, it will provide an opportunity for the young person to begin to tell their own story. This book is also for caregivers, mentors, teachers, and family members, for we need to hear the children's stories. Thank you, Donna, for writing and finishing your story. God will continue to use you and your experiences to impact the lives of many. Oh how the Lord has transformed you, my friend, into a way-beyond-average daughter of the King!

MELODIE BISSELL
National Children's Facilitator of
The Christian and Missionary Alliance Church in Canada
President and Founder of Winning Kids Inc.

—

The continued abuse of girls and young women in our world is a growing concern to those of us in ministry. Donna Dyck has written a creative journal as a tool for those involved in ministry to those who are victims or at risk. This creative journal is not designed to stand as a narrative in its own right, but rather to be a model and encouragement for girls to write their own story. I believe that it will encourage both faith and hope in those who read it and will be useful in the hands of those who seek to help those who suffer.

FRANKLIN PYLES, PRESIDENT
The Christian and Missionary Alliance in Canada

—

Confessions of a Not-So-Average Girl is very valuable to be used even as curriculum. For us, it allowed insight and a way to talk to the girls about the simple way that Jesus can be with them throughout their lives. Girls we've known for years opened up in ways that they hadn't before. I've seen a lot of Christian curriculum over the years, being a child and youth worker, and often we pass by it because it is geared toward "churched" or "church" children and youth. Our girls were able to relate to this book in many ways and I think it can go beyond culture to the heart of many girls and help them to have a realistic view of what it means to be a Christian—to trust and follow God through it all.

NANA GYABENG

The Scott Mission, Toronto, Ontario

Here are a few comments from the hard-to-reach girls of Scott Mission's program:

- "Mom/Dad fighting—yours was worse. I want to learn how to ask God to help my family."

- The story was helpful because "there is hope for life."

- "Inspired me to go to church and do things in life."

- "It made me know that I am not the only one whose father drinks."

- "It was very helpful and good, now I feel good and now I am more happy with myself. There are not many books like this one."

—

In reading *Confessions*, I laughed, cried, experienced heartache and hope. Donna Dyck's personal story, written using the ordinary everyday images of kittens, swings, swimming, boys and alcohol, will immediately help youth relate to this book. As she shares more deeply her story of an alcoholic home, feeling dumb, violence and loss, desperately wanting to fit in and feeling so alone, youth who have the undeveloped potential such as Donna had might begin to have hope for something more in their lives.

I applaud her ability to write simply—whether it is the concepts or the explanation of who God can be in their lives. Having ministered to inner city youth for years, I know there is not much out there that is written expressly *for* them. Donna has succeeded in giving them a tool that may help them experience a God that she held onto for years without a lot of understanding of who exactly He was. And so perhaps they can hold onto Him as well. Her questions may help them begin the journey of putting their unvoiced, squashed feelings into words.

This diary would also be a huge benefit to those working with inner city youth. It gives insight into how struggling youth think and serves well as a good introduction into their lives. I look forward to reading this book with some of the youth with whom I work and talking about some of the pain, joy and hopefulness that it elicits.

BETH WILTON

Work Force Director

Youth for Christ, Winnipeg, Manitoba

CONFESSIONS

of a Not-So-Average Girl

DONNA LEA DYCK

Journal

CONFESSIONS OF A NOT-SO-AVERAGE GIRL

ISBN: 978-1-77069-336-4

Printed in Canada.

Word Alive Press
131 Cordite Road, Winnipeg, MB R3W 1S1
www.wordalivepress.ca

Library and Archives Canada Cataloguing in Publication

Dyck, Donna Lea, 1960-

    Confessions of a not-so-average girl / Donna Lea Dyck.

ISBN 978-1-77069-336-4

    I. Title.

PS8607.Y34C66 2011   C813'.6   C2011-905537-6

This book is dedicated to the loving memory of my brother
Douglas Campbell McMartin
June 1960—July 2010

Acknowledgements

I would like to thank many dear friends and family who have encouraged and helped me in this project. You have all inspired and cheered for me. I thank each of you; my husband Bill, all my family, Susan Ponting, Judy Kirwin, Jason Hildebrand and Ernie Johannson. A special thanks to Melodie Bissell, who has very kindly taken me under her wing. Above all, I give thanks to my Saviour and best friend, Jesus, who walks with me always.

Sincerely,
Donna Lea Dyck

Introduction

I remember waking up one night seeing my pillow all lit up. I was sure it was an angel. I had heard about heavenly visits, but I never thought an angel would visit me. Well, as it turned out, what lit up my pillow that night wasn't an angel at all—it was a firefly!

Believing in angels is sort of like believing in God. I always believed in God—I just never thought He would care about a girl like me. I was considered the "queen of average." My school report cards were always pretty much the same: "Donna is an average girl." This summed up my feelings about myself.

When I was eight years old, I started writing in a diary. I knew my family was different from pretty much all my friends. Mom told me my dad was an alcoholic. I had to ask her what that was. She said it was someone who drinks too much. Living in my house was not always easy.

I know that I am not the only person who grew up in a messed up home. Everyone needs to find some way to deal with all the bad stuff that goes on. When my parents would fight and the beer bottles were smashing against the wall downstairs, you would often find me sitting in my bedroom closet. I was writing in my diary to my imaginary friend. The day came when I needed to find someone real to write to. I had heard a little about Jesus, so I chose Him. That is how we became best friends. He didn't make my life perfect but I found I had more peace. Take a look. Maybe there are some things you will discover in this diary that you can totally relate to.

Donna Lea Dyck

Chapter One

My Favourite Hiding Place

Dear Friend,

I need someone to talk to, so I picked you. I hope you don't mind. Recess was fun today. I love double-dutch skipping. I guess 'cause I'm good at it. I hope Daddy isn't late tonight. I sure get tired of that. The truth is, being a girl who does not like the dark makes it all worse if you ask me. When we are alone at night—just my sister Vandy, my little brother Doug, and me—it's just plain scary. I always think that something horrible is going to happen.

Sleeping with one eye open tonight!

Donna

What scares you?

❖ ❖

Dear Friend,

There was a big fight at school today. I had to pick sides. I hate that. I like all the girls, even the rich, smart ones. I couldn't believe they asked me to be on their side. It was so stupid. I didn't even know what the fight was about.

Today was the big race at school. Kathy Hill thought she would beat me by cutting halfway around the field. I still beat her. She might have nice clothes, but I can still run faster than her.

Love, Donna

Have you ever felt the way Donna felt here?

❖ ❖

Dear Friend,

Today I sat in a tree with my sister Vandy and our friend Gabby. We spied on our brothers. We caught them stealing candy and they had to give us most of it. A deal is a deal. I love pretending I am a private eye, the best one you could ever find. Well, I think we did well today. Those boys were sorry. Not me, though!

Goodnight, Donna

❖ ❖

Dear Friend,

What a gross way to start the day. Today Danny Marefield threw up all over his desk right behind me. I think he had eggs for breakfast. I will never eat eggs again.

Mom made lunch for me today. I told her that moms do that. I am not sure why my mom wouldn't have known this. When she makes my sandwich, it feels normal. If that's what normal is, I am not sure. I notice that kids who seem to have happy families have cleared-off kitchen tables with flowers or something in the centre, and moms who do things like make lunch for their kids. Mom never got mad at me when I told her this. She told me she never knew what kind of sandwich I wanted. I told her I didn't care. I just liked knowing she remembered I was coming home for lunch.

Mom said Susie (our cat) is going to have kittens. I love kittens. Hope she has them tomorrow.

Love, Donna

❖ ❖

Dear Friend,

You won't believe what happened today. I tried to find clean clothes, but couldn't. They were all too dirty, so I had to wear my ugly dress. What a gross dress—all yellow except for two buttons right where a girl wouldn't want them!

Even worse, I didn't wear underwear because they were dirty. Sitting down was not so great. I felt so embarrassed. I didn't tell anyone, that is for sure. I didn't play any sports today, either, because that would be really bad.

Everything was going okay 'til I walked home. We were not that far from school when Peter Bigtree ran up behind me and lifted my dress. So I turned around and gave him a BIG black eye. I think he got off easy, if you ask me. I guess a teacher saw us because he was right there asking what was going on. I had to go to the principal's office. Peter got in more trouble than me and that's what matters. I gotta learn how to do laundry.

Bad day.

Donna

Have you ever been embarrassed by your clothes, or something else maybe?

❖ ❖

Dear Friend,

Mrs. Smithson, who lives in the next townhouse from us, went crazy today. She was screaming out her window like a lunatic. She had one of those big kitchen knives and told us she'd come down and use it on us. I feel bad for her sons. It's gotta be embarrassing.

I saw Mr. Smithson and told him his wife was going crazy. He was walking really fast and didn't want to talk much.

Love, Donna

❖ ❖

Dear Friend,

Today was a fun day. Vandy, I, and some other kids went down the Hicks Hills in a barrel. Dad got this cardboard barrel and we stuffed it with blankets and rolled like crazy. It was so fun! I like it when Daddy gets weird stuff.

Love, Donna

❖ ❖

Dear Friend,

Mom and Dad are fighting a lot these days. I hate listening to them.

Mom says Dad drinks too much. She told me he's an alcoholic. I have never heard of that before. I always knew Dad was different. Grandma told me once that my dad was no good. I don't like her. She's mean. Dad is really smart. Mom told me he has two university degrees.

He drinks and smokes and swears, but he's still my dad and I love him.

Love, Donna

> *How do you feel when people in your house fight?*

❖ ❖

Dear Friend,

Today Dad took us kids to a town where there were corkscrew slides. Those are Vandy and Doug and my most favourite slides in the world. I like having my brother and sister all so close. My brother is seven and I am eight and Vandy is nine. I am the same height as Vandy. I like that.

My dad may be an alcoholic, but he sure is nice. He bought me pink popcorn today.

Love, Donna

❖ ❖

Dear Friend,

Today there was an open house at my school. My cousin Roger came to watch me work in the library. It was so nice of Roger. I am glad he came. I will never forget he did that for me.

Love, Donna

❖ ❖

Dear Friend,

Today I was thinking about how everyone in the world matters—except me. I feel invisible, if that makes sense, so I made a plan. I think that if I broke my leg, then people would notice me. It sounds painful, though, and I am not a big fan of pain.

I keep waiting for Susie, my lifetime favourite cat, to have kittens. She is my best friend. When I am sad and cry Susie licks my tears.

Love, Donna

Do you ever feel like you don't matter?

❖ ❖

Dear Friend,

I feel embarrassed. I don't know if I should tell my mom. I don't think she will believe me, plus I don't want to get in trouble again. Can I just tell you?

Today my dad was sitting in his chair. I was playing tag with Vandy and Doug. Dad leaned forward and called me over to him. He put his mouth on mine to kiss me and put his tongue in my mouth. It was so gross. I pulled away and ran upstairs. My heart is still beating so fast.

I am so mixed up.

From Donna

Do you know a real story like this? Who would be a safe person that Donna could have told?

❖ ❖
Dear Friend,

Today I took Simon to the park again. He lives in a house nearby. It is hard for me to believe we are the same age. His mom told me he is mentally handicapped and that's why he bangs his hands together and never talks. I don't like that he drools all the time though. I think it's gross. I know it's not his fault.

He likes the park. His mom really thanked me for being Simon's friend. I guess he doesn't have many. I bet life is hard for his mom.

I wonder why Simon is like that?

Love, Donna

❖ ❖
Dear Friend,

Sorry I didn't write for a while. Today was a big day and I had to tell you...

Susie had her kittens!

When I got home from school, Vandy and Doug were already home. They didn't know Susie had her babies, but she came right to me and meowed and so I followed her into Doug's room. She jumped into his dresser drawer and started licking her four beautiful babies! We phoned mom at the hospital where she works. A nurse told me Mom was telling all the other nurses what was happening with all the patients. It is called "report." I knew that a report is very important and that we were not allowed to phone mom then.

Some things are too important to wait! So when the nurse told me I needed to call back later, I told them it was a family emergency. I don't think she agreed with me, but it sure was to us. Finally, we got to speak to my mom. We said we wanted her to come home right away. She couldn't because she was just starting her shift. We were sad she couldn't come, but we sure had fun looking at the kittens!

Love, Donna

❖ ❖

Dear Friend,

I watched a lady on TV this week. She talked about God and miracles. Her face shone like an angel.

Today, I went and sat behind our townhouse in the ditch and thought about God. I don't know much about him. I want him to think I am good and I wish I could make Him happy. I'm just not sure how to do that.

Love, Donna

> *What do you think about God?*

❖ ❖

Dear Friend,

Today I went to the park by myself. I like swinging so high that the chain sags. That's when I leave all the things that are driving me crazy way below me. Then I jump off and see how far I can fly.

Usually this isn't a problem... but today was not one of those days. A boy left his bike near where I was swinging—I guess he thought it would be safe there. Well, it wasn't. When I jumped I landed on it and broke some of his spokes. He was pretty mad and started yelling at me. I told him he shouldn't have left his bike so close to the swings. He said it wasn't close. I told him it was when people are jumping off swings. He didn't seem to agree. I think I said sorry. I hope so. I really wasn't trying to be mean.

The flying princess, Donna

❖ ❖

Dear Friend,

Today Grandma died. My mom cried. I just couldn't. I thought Grandma was mean. She did buy me some cool pajamas and dresses for Christmas, which was nice of her, but I just don't like that she never thought much of my dad. I feel sad for my mom, but that's it.

The kittens opened their eyes today! They all have blue eyes. I am going to bring the kittens to school for show-and-tell soon. The kids will love the kittens. I hope Susie won't mind.

Love, Donna

What was it like for you when someone died?

❖ ❖

Dear Friend,

Dad is drunk tonight. I hate it when he's drunk. He acts so stupid. Dad thinks he is a philosophy major. It is so embarrassing—especially when he invites boys from my class into our house to talk. I don't know what they talk about and I don't care. I hate it.

Bad day.

Donna

What does a bad day look like for you?

❖ ❖

Dear Friend,

Ever since I started school, I have been in Group 3. Once I asked my teacher why I'm always in Group 3. She said it is because I am an average girl. I am not sure if she thought that would make me feel good. I noticed it is the group known pretty well as, ""The not-too-smart people." Maybe we are all the average kids, but that just doesn't seem right to me.

I asked my mom today when I got home from school, "Why am I with the Group 3 kids every year?" She said she thinks it's because I'm dyslexic. That means you get things backwards a lot when you read. That is true for me, especially when I'm nervous. At least that's what I think.

I might as well tell you, everyone else already knows—I am the worst speller in the class. A few weeks ago the teacher had to change the rules finally because I can never seem to get perfect on my spelling test. For the last three weeks she kept saying, "If everyone gets perfect on their spelling tests, I'll bring in a cake."

I am the only one who keeps getting two wrong. Now, the class is really mad at me. I study very hard. I even spell my whole list to my cat. She usually meows when I am done. I pretend she says, "That is very good, Donna."

Today the teacher changed the rules again. This time she said, "If everyone gets perfect, and Donna only gets one wrong, then I'll bake a cake for all of us."

I think the whole class has come up to me to warn me that I better only get one wrong!

I will try very hard. It is hard being dyslexic, or average, or whatever it is that I am.

From Donna

Do you or someone you know have a learning disability? How do you think it feels?

❖ ❖

Dear Friend,

I don't even want to go to school today. My dad was drunk when he went to parent-teacher interviews. If I could wear a bag on my head I would. What will my teacher think of me now? It is bad enough being in Group 3.

Bad day again.

Donna

❖ ❖

_____

_____

_____

_____

_____

_____

_____

_____

_____

_____

_____

_____

_____

_____

_____

_____

_____

_____

_____

_____

_____

_____

_____

_____

_____

_____

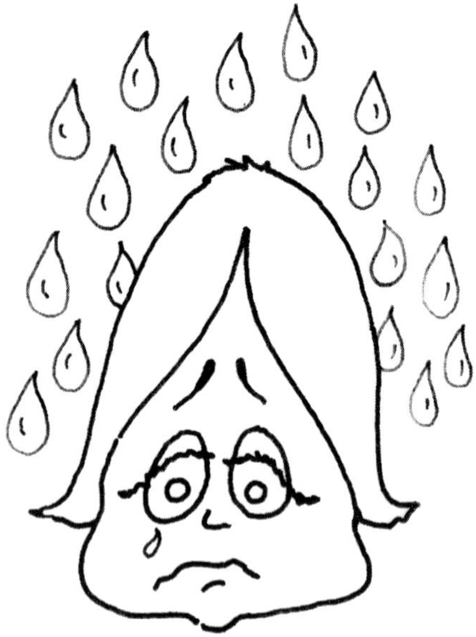

Chapter 2

A New Friend Sometimes Makes All the Difference

Dear Jesus,

My girlfriend, Gabby, says you're God's Son. I thought I would write to you instead. I sure hope you don't mind.

Mom and Dad are fighting again tonight. I hate it when Mom throws beer bottles against the wall. I just feel scared. That is why I am writing in my closet today.

I love sitting in this closet even if it is a little crowded with my pillow, blankets and my lamp. It feels safe now, and I like that.

I'm glad I can talk to you, Jesus. I need someone bigger than me.

Love, Donna

Who do you talk to when your life is falling apart?

❖ ❖

Dear Jesus,

I am tired today. I didn't sleep well last night. I was scared. I tried to sleep with Vandy, and held onto her nightgown so that if someone tried to steal me, I would know. Vandy kicked me out of her bed. So I tried my brother and found out that he still wets the bed.

I don't think I will sleep with him again!

At night, I feel very alone and scared. I don't know what to do.

Love, Donna

❖ ❖

Dear Jesus,

My mom took me to the doctor today. He says I am anemic. Now, I have to drink this horrid black stuff. It tastes like car oil.

Today, I found my Christmas present. It is a cherry red accordion with lots and lots of buttons. I begged my mom for it. Every Christmas Vandy and Doug and I study the Sears Christmas flyer, and that's where I found my greatest wish. Mom really needs to learn who she is hiding these gifts from. I am a very good present-finder. It was in the hall closet. Now, I play it when no one is home. I play in the closet. It just seems a safer spot in case someone comes. I hope I'll get really good one day. I will have to act surprised on Christmas morning.

Love, Donna

❖ ❖

Dear Jesus,

Just for the record, I got only one wrong on my spelling test. I am not sure if you help kids with stuff like that. In case you do, I just want to say thank you. That was a hard test, and everyone was looking at me. At least it felt like that. The whole class cheered for me when I got only one wrong! They all got perfect, of course… which bugs me.

Love, Donna

❖ ❖

Dear Jesus,

I tasted beer today. It is gross. I don't understand how people can drink it!

Now all the kittens sleep with me at night. There is hardly any room for me. At least I feel a little safer now.

I was so mad on Sunday. Dad took us three kids to an outdoor rink to skate. He dropped us off and said he would be back in a while. It was fun at first. Then it got colder and darker. There were no kids left. All the other parents came and picked up their kids. I wondered if he was ever coming back. We sat there freezing to death. Finally, he came. He said he went to the bar for a few drinks. I guess he forgot us.

I don't think all dads are like this. How did I get stuck with my dad? Do you forget people, Jesus?

Love, Donna

> *Have you ever been left behind?*
> *How did you feel about it?*

❖ ❖

Dear Jesus,

Did you see the cool teeter-totter my dad built in the basement? It's huge! We give each other amazing bumps. Today, I think we went a bit too far. Vandy and I asked Doug to get on one end and we sat on the other. We were bumping him pretty good. But that last one didn't just bump him... it shot him into the air and onto the hard basement floor. When he finally landed we told him he was a fabulous flying star! We didn't want to get in trouble. We told Doug he'd be famous one day. He didn't cry too much. I was glad.

Christmas is almost here. I like Christmas. Soon, I won't have to play my accordion in the closet.

Love, Donna

❖ ❖

Dear Jesus,

I can't believe the way some people lie! About a month ago, Gail told Vandy that her dad was dead. We felt sorry for her. Then today when Gail was at our house playing dolls with us, her mom called and said her dad was coming over to pick her up so they could go out for supper. So, we told her mom that Gail told us her real dad was dead. She said, "No he's not." Why would someone tell a lie like that? Vandy and I were shocked. It bugs me because we felt so sorry for her—the little faker.

Tonight Vandy and I built a home for the kittens out of a box we found. We even made couches and beds for them. Vandy and I are pretty creative if you ask me. We made furniture out of margarine tubs and tissue boxes. We used up all of mom's facecloths because they were the kitten's blankets. The kittens weren't too wild about the idea of blankets, but hopefully they will get used to it. We can't seem to keep them in their beds! They may have to keep sleeping with me. That's better anyway, because with them around I just sleep better!

I think tomorrow Vandy and I will make the kittens some clothes out of some old socks. I already have some great ideas.

Love, Donna

❖ ❖

Dear Jesus,

Christmas was mostly good. I couldn't believe Dad started drinking as soon as we finished opening our presents. He has never done that before on Christmas. Mom said he couldn't come with us to my Aunt's house for Christmas Dinner. Dad gets into bad fights with my uncle when he drinks. It is embarrassing. We left him at home. I did feel bad leaving Dad, but I was mad at him, too. I like my accordion. I made sure to look really surprised!

I heard Christmas is supposed to be your birthday, Jesus. I never knew that. Happy birthday!

Love, Donna

> *Did you know that Christmas is the day we celebrate Jesus birthday? What do you know about Jesus?*

❖ ❖

Dear Jesus,

I know it's been a while since I wrote to you. Jesus, I am pretty sure you are real.

When Daddy asked me to go to Montreal with him, I was so surprised. We had to go fix up the house my parents owned there so we could sell it. Dad and I painted it yellow. That was the good part, Jesus.

The bad part was when Daddy started drinking and then we had to start driving back to Ontario. Jesus, I am wondering, do you know how to drive? When Daddy turned off onto the ramp, the car was hitting the guardrail a whole bunch of times. I really thought I was gonna die. You must have seen me praying really hard in the back seat. All of a sudden the car was driving straight. I don't think it was because of Daddy, because he was way too drunk and his driving got better way too fast.

Thanks, Jesus, for coming with me. I was pretty scared.

Your friend still, Donna

Have you ever felt like God kept you safe?

❖ ❖

Dear Jesus,

I don't even know what to think today. I worked so hard to learn how to play my accordion. I know I wasn't that good at it.

When I was at school today, Dad stayed home and got drunk. When I got home, I went upstairs to play my accordion and I couldn't find it anywhere. I asked Dad about it, and he said he gave it to the boy next door. I couldn't believe it.

I will never play an instrument again.

I just cried with my cat. I can't believe my dad would give my favourite gift away.

Love, Donna

❖ ❖

Dear Jesus,

I have cried so hard, I don't think I will be able to cry again for at least a week. Today the superintendent came and tried to take away our cat. My sister and brother and I were all in the bathroom watching him and crying our eyes out. I am sure you must have heard us, Jesus—I think all the neighbors did. My dad sure heard us. He went outside and grabbed the superintendent and held him against the lamppost so his feet were not even touching the ground. Dad yelled at him so loudly, the man went away without our cat. I think Dad scared him. I know he will be back. He has taken everyone's cat in the all the townhouses. He is very mean if you ask me.

At least we have the cat for a little while more.

Love, Donna

Do you know anyone mean like this Superintendent in your life? Why do you think they are like that?

❖ ❖

_____

_____

_____

_____

_____

_____

_____

_____

_____

Chapter 3

Stuff Happens, Sometimes We Like It, and Sometimes We Don't

Dear Jesus,

Can you hear Mom and Dad fighting again? I hate it when they fight. I'm so glad I can sit in my closet and write to you. Mom must be really mad, because she's throwing beer bottles at the wall again.

This is scary, Jesus.

I hope you don't mind me writing to you. I don't think anyone really cares what it's like in my house.

At school I always feel bad about being me. I see the other girls. They have nice clothes and straight hair. People say my curly hair is beautiful. Mom always says to eat my crusts and I'll have curly hair. I don't want curly hair. So I don't eat my crusts anymore.

Wow, Jesus, they are still fighting. It feels so scary. I wish they'd stop.

Love, Donna

> *What scares you? Who do you talk to when you're scared?*

❖ ❖

Dear Jesus,

Remember the fight my mom and dad had the other day? It must have been pretty bad, 'cause Mom told me today that Dad and my brother are moving to British Columbia. Dad is going to find a job there.

Mom said she gave Dad a choice—to stop drinking or leave.

I guess Dad chose to keep drinking, because he's leaving before the summer begins.

Mom told me Doug was going to go with him. She can't afford to keep all three of us kids and thinks it may be better for Doug. I don't feel too good about that idea. I bet Mom is finding it hard, too. Mom said we are moving to an apartment near us. It has a pool. That is the good news, plus we are going to live on the tenth floor. The view from the balcony should be good. I have never lived in an apartment before. I think the elevator rides will be cool, too! I am trying to think about the good things, if you are wondering.

I feel sad that Dad is leaving though. I can't even think about what it will be like when he and Doug are gone.

How can a dad choose beer over his family?

Love, Donna

> *Can you describe the feelings someone has when their parents split up?*

❖ ❖

Dear Jesus,

Dad and Doug are gone now. I asked Mom again why she sent Doug with Dad. She said she thought Dad needed some responsibility. I still don't know if that was a good idea. It is weird not having them here.

Jesus, I wish Mom and Dad could figure things out. I hate when they fight, but I really don't like that he is gone. I wish we could be a normal family.

I wish with my whole heart I could make Dad stop drinking. I tried cleaning the house and begging him. Nothing worked. Mom says an alcoholic has to *want* to stop drinking. That was so frustrating to find out. I am wondering, Jesus, can make people stop drinking? Could you look at my dad? Maybe you can make him stop. That would be very nice of you.

Our new apartment is okay. We live on the tenth floor. I found out that Elly Fisher lives across the hall from me. I hope she will be my friend. I have known her since grade one. Now I am going into grade six.

I really like the pool. It's huge. I'm going to get an amazing tan this summer. You will see, Jesus.

Our cat likes to sleep on the railing of our balcony. How can a cat sleep there and not fall off? I can barely get the courage to stand close enough to the railing just to look over, let alone sleep on it. I think the cat is a bit nuts.

Well, I am going swimming now. Bye.

Love, Donna

> *What are the qualities that make up a best friend?*

❖ ❖

Dear Jesus,

Here is what I want to know. I have this new friend and her name is Mary. I really like her. She plays with dolls, though. The truth is, I love dolls. I just don't tell people. My favourite is my doll Patty. I always make sure she is sick or we are going on a trip. I am very good at making clothes for her. I like to use socks. My mom can't figure out why I have no socks. She just needs to look at my doll. It becomes clear pretty fast.

What I am not sure about is, is it okay to play dolls when you are going into grade six? Mary and I, we had a great time and all, I just don't want people to find out. It could be embarrassing.

Love, Donna

❖ ❖

Dear Jesus,

There are a lot of babysitting jobs in this apartment. Sometimes when I am on the elevator, parents of young kids ask my sister Vandra and I a million questions. I am pretty sure I know why they're asking us. They are looking for a babysitter.

I have to say that having a swimming pool right downstairs is pretty cool. I love swimming. Mom got Vandy and me nice swimsuits—mine is powder blue and Vandra's is green. I like mine better.

Love, Donna

❖ ❖

Dear Jesus,

Today, Vandy and I went and caught grasshoppers in a jar. I was thinking grasshopper hotel. At the start of the day it was fun. After an hour or so of catching, it grossed me out. Those bugs have big eyes and antennas. I let all mine go. I don't think I am going to be doing that again any time soon. I have to say though, God, you are really creative. I think grasshoppers are one of your stranger creations.

There are a lot of kids in this building. Even some cute boys!

Love, Donna

❖ ❖

Dear Jesus,

I don't like grade six. No one wants to be my friend. At least, that is how it seems. Everyone I know is in the other class. I feel like a total loser. My teacher isn't nice. She got mad at me because I rolled my eyes. I just thought tapping the ruler while we sang the anthem was weird.

I don't think fitting in would be that hard. If I could own a pair of jeans that look like the other girls' in my class it might help.

If all this isn't bad enough, our apartment has cockroaches. I think they are the grossest, ugliest, biggest bugs on the planet. I am not happy about this at all. I am going to get rid of them. I am making plans already.

Bye, Donna

> *Do you feel like you don't fit in? How important is it to have the right clothes and look a certain way?*

Dear Jesus,

Mom is making Vandy and I go to Alateen. It is for teenagers who have a mom or dad who is an alcoholic.

Well, Jesus, I am only eleven. They told me I am supposed to be twelve to be there. I guess they think I am mature for my age. It has to be true. I am doing all the laundry now. Mom made that my new chore. I don't mind, though. When the superintendent saw me doing laundry, he told me I was too young. I said that I agreed, but he would have to talk to my mom. So he did. Mom told him that I did a better job than my older sister and it was safer to have me do it. I confess I was proud in a strange kind of way.

Alateen is kind of weird. Some of the kids are nice. I met one nice girl. She seemed to like me okay. Her name is Marjory. The kids there all smoke a lot. I could hardly breathe.

Love, Donna

❖ ❖

Dear Jesus,

They told me at Alateen that my dad's drinking is his problem and not mine. I guess that is supposed to make me feel better.

It's not working so far.

Bye, Donna

Do you ever feel like other people's problems are your fault? Do you think that is the truth?

❖ ❖

Dear Jesus,

I like the new prayer I learned at Alateen. It goes like this:

"God grant me the serenity to accept the things I cannot change, courage to change the things I can and wisdom to know the difference. Amen."

This prayer is about knowing what I can change and what I can't. I can't change Dad or stop him from drinking, even though I want to. The only person I can change is me.

Jesus, I know I need to change some stuff. I hope you can help me. I tried to make people feel sorry for me. That didn't work. So, now I'm going to think of something new.

Love, Donna

> What kind of stuff do you think
> you need to change?

❖ ❖

Dear Jesus,

I was so surprised when Elly Fisher knocked on my door. She wants to be my friend! I thought she hated me, because she usually didn't talk to me.

So, now I have one friend. Elly has pretty, long, straight brown hair and big brown eyes. She has a nice mother and father. They have really good food at her house. Her mom makes us macaroni and cheese and really good spaghetti. I think we are going to be really good friends. We laugh a lot.

I sure like recess, Jesus. I am good at double-dutch and jumpsies. Maybe you saw me?

Love, Donna

Dear Jesus,

Elly and I started hanging out with the cool kids. They smoke, though. We tried it. It's not my favourite. Chocolate bars are way better. You look cooler smoking than you do eating chocolate bars, Jesus. I thought it was kinda weird how we tried holding the cigarettes in different ways, trying to figure out what looked the coolest.

I have my first crush on... well... two boys. But I know they won't like me.

Did you notice, though, that Bobby Hill and I are both left-handed? He asked me if he could borrow my baseball glove. That made me happy!

Love, Donna

P. S. Mom bought me jeans and a purple raincoat from the Sears flyer. It is the nicest coat in my whole class.

> *What have you done to try to make friends and fit in?*

Dear Jesus,

There are a lot of fights going on.

Today I felt so stupid. Sherry-Lee, the prettiest, best-dressed, smartest girl at school told me that I am clueless because I don't watch hockey. I hate feeling dumb.

I am good at drawing, though, and I can run fast—faster than her, and I'm glad about that!

I miss my dad and brother, Jesus. I wish they could come home.

Love, Donna

> *When have you ever felt*
> *dumb, like Donna did?*

❖ ❖

Dear Jesus,

I am not at all happy about Christmas without Dad and Doug. I really like the clothes Mom bought me. It is a lot of pink, though. I am not quite sure how I feel about a pink top, pink sweater and a pink skirt. But it sure matches!

We did have fun at my Aunt's on Christmas day. We always have an amazing Turkey dinner. She sure is a good cook. We play a lot of games. I really like winning. My mom says I like it a little too much.

Elly and I got these plastic things you tie onto your boots, sort of like short skis. They are a lot of fun. Sadly, you can't steer too good with them. Just ask my friend Elly. We decided to give these things a try. There is a hill right beside the apartment building. It is not that it is so long, but it is steep. You get some good speed on these plastic things. Elly went first. She was flying down the hill and aimed poorly. She smashed into the corner of the apartment building. I went flying down to rescue her. There was not much I could do. She developed a big bruise down the middle of her body. It looked pretty painful. I confess, it was pretty funny, though.

Love, Donna

Dear Jesus,

One of the newest things Elly and Vandy and I do is hang out in the hallway on the tenth floor of our building. We bring our radio and play our favourite music as loud as our neighbors allow us. Sometimes the guys from the other floors come and hang out with us. We are all close in age. We are a big group when you get us all together. Vandy has a crush on at least one of the boys. Not me, though. Sometimes we play soccer in the hall, but the neighbors are not very wild about that idea.

It is a lot of fun, I confess.

Love, Donna

_____

_____

_____

_____

_____

_____

_____

_____

_____

_____

_____

_____

_____

_____

_____

_____

_____

_____

Chapter 4

Young Girl Goes to Church

Dear Jesus,

Did you notice that I have a detention every day after school?

I can't believe it myself. I know I am innocent. Mr. Stevens says he needs company after school. I seem to be his favourite company. There are lots of other kids, though. I am not the only one, but it seems I am there the most. He is always joking around with all of us. He helps me with math and science. He is such a nice man. He must know that my dad is gone.

I wonder what it would be like to have a dad like him. My friend, Elly, has to be careful because if Mr. Stevens sees her waiting for me, he gives her a detention too. One day he made her do a math problem: 123456789 x 987654321. Then she had to prove her answer through long division. Elly is very careful not to let Mr. Stevens see her now!

I am worried about my sister Vandy. Mom says she is depressed. It is hard not having Dad and Doug home. I try not to think about it.

Love, Donna

Do you have people in your family who seem depressed? How does that make you feel?

❖ ❖

Dear Jesus,

I have been very busy. I am finally in grade seven. Now, we all go to a new school. I have quite a few friends. They all smoke and some like drugs and drinking. I don't like that stuff. I only smoked a bit last year. But I think it's stupid. I definitely don't want to drink or do drugs—that would be even "stupider!"

Elly and I decided that we want to go to church. There is one down the road. We are going to walk there. I hope they don't get mad because I don't have a dress... at least not one I want to wear in front of people. I will wear pants. I have one pair of dress pants. I hope girls are allowed to wear pants in church. Elly has nice dresses. Her mom told me once it is because they only have Elly to buy for. Her brothers are way older than her. That is okay. Elly never makes me feel bad. At least I can use my babysitting money to buy jeans and stuff now. Vandy and I always share clothes. It is like having twice as many clothes, except you really don't.

Love, Donna

> *How could going to church be helpful to someone?*

❖ ❖

Dear Jesus,

Church was nice and the people sure seemed happy. The people there were all dressed up. I was so glad to see that guy with long hair wearing a beer t-shirt. His jeans were ripped, too. Maybe you saw him?

I don't remember what they taught me, but they were really nice to Elly and me.

We are going to go back.

Love, Donna

❖ ❖

Dear Jesus,

My mom isn't too happy about me going to church. She says that the church is full of hypocrites. I don't know exactly what those are, Jesus. I checked when I was in church, but all I saw were a lot of nice people. They were really happy, too!

I think it is sad. I know that churches are not full of perfect people. I checked it out last week. They are just people. Some seem more messed up than others. I wish Mom would give them another chance.

Elly's parents are not very happy that we're going to church, either—mostly her dad. But we are still going to go. We are joining Junior Word of Life. That is for kids our age. The other kids there are really nice. We are going to have a lot of fun.

Love, Donna

Have you ever gone to a Youth Group at a church? Is there one you could check out?

❖ ❖

Dear Jesus,

When I went to church today, we sang this song. I am sure you heard it. I really liked it and it made sense to me.

"*Something beautiful, something good, all my confusion, you understood. All I had to offer him was brokenness and strife, but he made something beautiful of my life.*"

Thank you for caring about me, Jesus.

Love, Donna

Is there something in this song that makes sense to you?

❖ ❖

Dear Jesus,

I didn't like Christmas much this year. Dad and Doug were not here. Mom says Doug is coming back soon, though. He is missing Mom (and hopefully us, too).

I am thankful for friends and for my Sunday school teacher. She gave me green hangers for Christmas. They are nice.

Love, Donna

P.S. My mom says Doug is coming home soon. He wrote her and asked if he could please come home. I am glad he is coming back. Mom seems happy, too.

Love, Donna

❖ ❖

Dear Jesus,

You know Chris who lives down the hall from me? He is in the same grade as Vandy. We have hung out with him a lot these past few months. This morning when we were leaving for school, our neighbors told us that his mom was brutally murdered in the underground parking garage!

Donna and I didn't know what to say when Chris called us to walk to school with him. He didn't say anything about his poor mom. We went down the elevator to the lobby and there were police everywhere. We were not allowed to go out the back way.

I was so scared, Jesus.

Chris made up a story and told us a little puppy dog died—and that someone threw the puppy down the stairs. We knew the truth, though. I think Chris just couldn't face it. I don't blame him, Jesus.

When we were in class, they called Elly, Vandy and me to go down to the counselor's office with Chris. They wanted us to be there when they told Chris that his mom had died.

Oh Jesus, I just didn't know what to say to him. We walked home with Chris and his dad was waiting for him. I didn't even know he had a dad. We never saw him before.

Jesus, what will Chris and his brother and sister do now? Why do such bad things happen?

Love, Donna

> *Have you ever been in a really bad and sad situation? What happened?*

❖ ❖

Dear Jesus,

I learned at church that I could ask you anything. I heard that you could do really hard things. So … I'd like to ask you for my next year's Christmas present. I want you to bring my dad back home.

I can't stand him being alone so far away, even if he is drunk.

I like having Doug home. I know he is glad to be home. His suitcase was full of all kinds of turn-of-the-century bottles. I guess they are antiques. He also had these cool beads that look super ancient. He said he and Dad found them. He didn't have too much in the way of clothes, though. Mom had to take him shopping and get some so he could go to school the next day.

Love, Donna

> *What would be a hard thing to ask God to do for you or your family?*

❖ ❖

Dear Jesus,

Vandy is really having a bad day. She was at her boyfriend's apartment on the third floor of our building. When they looked out, they could not believe what they saw. A lady falling through the air. She must have jumped from a balcony way above. Vandy and her friend ran to the ground where she was laying. Vandy said the lady threw up and then died. They are going to have nightmares for sure.

Life must be very bad for some people. She must have needed a friend really badly.

Love, Donna

❖ ❖

Dear Jesus,

Thank you for my friends and for my surprise birthday party! I couldn't believe it. I also couldn't believe that Mr. Stevens kept me after school even though it was my birthday. I told him that I wasn't very impressed and that I was innocent. I was so good all day.

I found out Vandy and Elly asked him to keep me late. He was delighted to help.

That was very nice to have that party, Jesus.

Thank you for my sister and all my friends.

Love, Donna

❖ ❖

Dear Jesus,

I love summer. I think it is my favourite season. I hope it is super sunny!

I like babysitting Sarah, Emily and Janet. I like having a job during the week. This way I am not bored and I get to buy a new pair of jeans and maybe a top in September.

The girls are really good. We swim a lot. They are easy to get along with.

I like roller-skating, too. It's fun. I think I am pretty good at it. Maybe you noticed? I finally figured out how to dance on roller skates.

There are some cute boys there. I hope they are impressed with my dancing abilities. I'd check to see if they noticed, but I am afraid I will fall and that would be too embarrassing. It takes a lot of concentration!

I had a talk with my mom last night. Now I think I understand why she hates churches. She told me when she and Dad were first married, a minister counseled them, because Dad's drinking was already driving her nuts. He said if he was married to a woman like her, he would drink, too. I didn't know what to say to her. I don't think he was a very good minister.

Love, Donna

> *This one minister gave bad advice to Donna's mom. How do you know when you receive bad advice?*

❖ ❖

Dear Jesus,

Did you see my two black eyes? I got the first one last night when I ran into the bedroom door. Vandy and I share a double bed and she threw up right beside me. (You know that I am not too good with the throwing-up thing.) So I jumped out of bed and ran straight into the edge of the door with my eye first. I thought it was open all the way. My eye turned black really fast.

I got the second one the next day when I got hit by a baseball. Elly and I were playing catch together and I wasn't paying attention. She said I was looking at the boys, but I wasn't. I didn't know eyes could turn so black. In fact, my eyes are now officially black, blue and red. Wow, I look so ugly!

Elly and her mom took me to the hospital. What a long wait at the emergency! When the nurse asked me what colour my eyes were she didn't think it was very funny when I said, "Black." I can't believe how big the goose egg over my eye is! They didn't know if I was a boy or a girl. I don't think my short hairdo is working for me.

When the doctor finally came, he had a huge needle in his hand. I thought he was teasing me at first. He said he had to get some of the ketchup out of there so there would be less pain. He stuck it into my huge goose egg! I was surprised it didn't hurt that much. It looked BIG and BAD, though.

What a bad day. People kept staring at me. I think I've heard every black-eye joke on the planet.

Love, Donna

Have you ever felt like the whole world was staring at you? Why?

❖ ❖

_____

_____

_____

_____

_____

_____

_____

_____

_____

Chapter 5

Asking Jesus about the Big Stuff

Dear Jesus,

Today in Sunday school I heard that there is a "rule"—at least, that's the way it sounds to me. The teacher has been telling me I need to say this special prayer, so that You will live in my heart. I don't really get this whole idea because I thought we were already friends, and I don't want to stop having You as my friend. So, Jesus, just in case, I want to pray that prayer they told me. I hope I get it all right and don't leave out anything. If I do forget something, can You please keep being my friend anyway, Jesus?

Dear Jesus, so, I want to tell You I am sorry for the bad things I have done and anything that has made You sad. Please forgive me. And, Jesus, thank You for dying on the cross for me. I want You to be my real Saviour. I'm not sure what a Saviour is, but they told me that is who You are and I am okay with that. I still really need You to be my friend and to be with me all the time just in case this is different than being my Saviour.

Thank You, Jesus.

Love, Donna

P.S. I also found out that from now on, whenever I write about "You," I should use a capital letter. Sorry about that Jesus, I never heard that before.

> *Have you ever asked Jesus to be your best friend and your Saviour?*

❖ ❖

Dear Jesus,

I learned in Sunday school, that I should read my Bible every day. I love my Bible. Elly gave it to me. I picked the Psalms. I will read one Psalm a day. Please help me to understand it, I know it is important.

Donna

> *Do you have a Bible? Who gave it to you? What do you read that helps you and even makes your heart peaceful?*

❖ ❖

Dear Jesus,

Grade eight is better in some ways—like not having as many detentions, for one! Thank you for my newest friend, Cynthia. I told her about You, Jesus.

She invited me to her house. Her mom likes cleaning a lot and likes it when I come, because I guess I'm pretty messy. I spilled a few things by accident and she seemed very happy about it. Yesterday, when we went to her place after school, her mom was cleaning out all of her kitchen cupboards inside and out and was pretty proud of herself.

I never knew you were supposed to clean inside your cupboards. Cynthia asked me to go to her track club. She thinks I am a good runner. Maybe I will go sometime.

Love, Donna

❖ ❖

Dear Jesus,

I just wanted to remind You that Christmas is coming. I am hoping You will send Dad back to us. I know You can do anything. I'll be watching for him. Mom isn't very happy with me for praying like this.

Oh well... too late.

Love, Donna

> *Are you asking God for anything hard these days?*

❖ ❖

Dear Jesus,

Thank You for answering the biggest prayer of my life so far. I couldn't believe my eyes when I saw

Dad walk off the elevator. It has been over two years since I saw him.

It is good to have him home again.

You really can do hard things, Jesus. Thank You for caring about the stuff I pray about.

Love, Donna

❖ ❖

Dear Jesus,

I learned in Sunday school that You always protect me and help me. Thank you for babysitting with me on New Year's Eve.

Frank, a friend of the family I am babysitting for, is really creepy, Jesus. I was alone with the kids when he came back to the house around midnight. I knew something was weird. I didn't want to open the door, but he said he came to pick up his gloves that he left there and he had a big box of Smarties for me. I really like Smarties. I thought maybe I was being stupid for thinking the worst about him. I quickly found out that I wasn't.

My heart started pounding the moment I even slightly opened the door. He kicked the door and forced his way into the house. He kind of disappeared for a minute so I phoned my mom. I told her that there was a man in the house and that he might hurt me. I asked her to please send Dad over. Frank saw me hang up the phone and asked me who I called. I told him I called my mom to tell her that he was here. I also told him that my dad was on his way over (I didn't tell him we didn't have a car and it would take Dad at least an hour to get there.)

Then the awful man wanted me to kiss him. He put his arm around me. The kiss made me want to throw up. He is SO weird! I sure was praying hard. I got away from him and woke up one of the kids so I wouldn't have to be alone with him. I was desperate!

Eventually, I had to put poor Lucy back to bed—I just couldn't keep her awake. I tried hard not to act like I was terrified. Then he wanted to kiss me again. I don't know if I will ever like kissing. So far I think it is pretty gross.

All of a sudden, he asked me if I wanted him to leave.

I said, "Yes, I do!" He did. I couldn't believe it.

After he left, I went and checked all the doors in the house. He had unlocked every door! So I locked them all again. Then Dad came in the taxi and asked me where the man was. I showed him where he was sitting in his car just down the street. Dad ran to his car, but he took off.

Dad slept on the couch while we waited for the parents to come home. When they did, I told them about Frank and they didn't believe me! Why would I lie? At least Dad and Mom believed me.

Jesus, I hope I never see him again. Thank You for keeping me safe. I know it could have been worse.

Love, Donna

> *When have you been really scared? What happened? Do you ever pray for wisdom in a scary situation?*

❖ ❖
Dear Jesus,

So there is a cute guy hanging around with all my friends at the apartment. He has brown hair and nice brown eyes. I found out he really likes me. I am not too sure what to do about it. He wants me to be his girlfriend. The problem is, he will want me to kiss him. I don't know how, and I'm sure I still won't like it, even if it is him. I am not sure just what to say.

Love, Donna

❖ ❖
Dear Jesus,

It was so cool—my youth leader phoned Elly and me and asked us if we could go to their place on Friday and play games. I am so excited.

Good day,

Donna

> *When is a time that someone has invited you to their home and shown you kindness? How did this make you feel?*

❖ ❖

Dear Jesus,

You know how I had a boyfriend? Well, now I don't. It didn't last long. I forgot to mention him to You before. He isn't very interesting. He did have great brown eyes, though. He's gone now, anyway. Dad really didn't like him. I didn't tell Dad this boy takes drugs.

It doesn't matter now. I told Dad I won't date until I am 18. That is okay. I haven't seen many interesting guys—except at church, and those boys wouldn't be interested in me.

I just wanted You to know what was going on with me, Jesus.

Love, Donna

> *Do you hang out with people who you know are not really the best choice for you? How can you make better decisions about your relationships?*

❖ ❖

Dear Jesus,

I am still steaming mad. Did you hear my dad call me a slut? He was so nice to my friend, the one who is a little too friendly with boys. I am the one who doesn't even like kissing! Then, if all this isn't bad enough, my drunk dad said I would "never amount to anything." At least my dad was drunk, it would hurt more if he was sober.

Jesus, what am I supposed to do with this stuff?

Love, Donna

❖ ❖

Dear Jesus,

I couldn't believe what happened today. Cynthia, who I think has a pretty perfect life, says she wishes she could be like me! I think she's nuts.

She interviewed me for our school assignment. The teacher told us to choose someone we would like to be. I chose a movie star. I looked around our classroom and honestly couldn't see anyone I wanted to be. I know my life isn't perfect, but I actually don't mind being me. I don't get the point of this assignment anyway—you can't switch lives with another person, so why even bother thinking about it? What a completely dumb assignment.

Oh, I forgot to tell You, I got kicked out of music class today. I didn't like the clarinet anyway. So now I'm in a singing class. It isn't going so well. The teacher says I am distracting the class.

I never noticed.

Love, Donna

❖ ❖

Dear Jesus,

Another great day! Elly and I went over to our Youth Leader's home and we had a great time. We played games, drank pop and ate chips. It was great!

In church, we sing, "I'm so glad I am part of the family of God!" It seemed a bit weird to me to sing that, but I guess now I really am part of this big family.

Love, Donna

> What do you think it means to
> be part of God's family?

❖ ❖

Dear Jesus,

Grade eight is fun. I cannot tell You how much I am looking forward to summer, though I didn't survive singing class too well. The teacher asked me to leave and not come back. She said I am too distracting.

I must say I am good in the remedial class. They help me with Math and English. That is good, because I am not the best at either of them. I wish I was smart. The teachers are nice. I can tell they drink coffee a lot, not that I see them drink it or anything, but I can smell it when they lean over to help me.

When Elly and I left school today, some kids grabbed us and threw us on the ground and sat on top of us. There were so many of them and only two of us. They made us smoke their stupid cigarettes while they sat on us. What a bunch of bullies. That isn't easy to do, let me tell You. I could hardly breathe, let alone smoke! That was really gross. I thought they were going to beat us up. I am so glad that Susie's mom was driving by and saw us. She honked her horn and asked if we wanted a ride. The kids jumped off us and we ran like crazy and jumped in her car. You must have sent her, Jesus. Thank You. We were really scared.

Love, Donna

❖ ❖

Dear Jesus,

Summer is finally here. I wish it didn't go so fast. The girls I babysit are really nice. We swim a lot. I still like roller skating. I think I am getting better. The boys at the rink are still cute.

Please help Dad find a job, God. He really needs one. Mom and Dad started fighting again.

Love, Donna

❖ ❖

Dear Jesus,

Thank You for a really neat day. We went on a long bike ride along the river. It was so much fun. When we rode up on our bikes, there was a tire swing hanging over the river. I had never been on a tire swing before. I have to say I was a little surprised when I let go of the tire and landed on the roof of a car under the water. I had no idea there was a car there. I sure am glad I didn't go through the windshield. That would have been very bad.

Thank You for good friends and sunny days. I really like my bike. I bought it with some of my babysitting money. Forest green is not the coolest bike color.

Oh well, it works and I am thankful for it. I feel like Dorothy from Wizard of Oz. Her bike looked like mine. I don't have a basket, though.

Love, Donna

❖ ❖

Chapter 6

"Grow'n up is hard to do"...

Dear Jesus,

Today was the first day of grade nine. I can't believe I am in high school now! My day started okay. I have to tell You, though, it was hard to decide what to wear. I didn't want to stand out or look weird, so it took quite awhile to decide.

Finally, I made up my mind what clothes to wear, and Elly and I left for our first day of high school together. After that, the day got weird and really bad—fast.

When Elly and I went down the elevator, it stopped on the second floor. There were two ambulance guys standing there. I saw a lady on a stretcher and she was grayish blue. Then I saw Mr. Kemp, he's the father of the girls I babysat all summer. He was standing there really casually with two police officers on either side of him. He wasn't handcuffed. He said, "Hi," to me as we walked off the elevator. We were asked by the ambulance guys to get off so they could bring this lady on. So, of course we did. Then we got to the lobby and Elly and I went on to school. I didn't know what was going on. Later, I found out that Mr. Kemp strangled his wife and she died. Now he's in prison or will be really soon. I don't know what will happen to their little girls.

This is awful, Jesus. They said he thought she was cheating on him. She didn't seem like the cheating kind to me.

Love, Donna

> *Can you tell Jesus something that you will never forget because it was horrible? What happened?*

❖ ❖

Dear Jesus,

I don't like church these days. It seems kind of boring and people's lives seem a little too perfect for me. I think I will take a break. Elly said that she would be praying for me. That bugged me.

I will keep talking to You, Jesus. I like having You to talk to. I think I feel more peaceful on the inside, or something like that. One thing is for sure, just because I know You, it doesn't mean my life is without problems. I do like having You as my friend.

I can't believe how many kids at my school are mixed up. A lot of them have been in school with me since grade one. It really bugs me how they are so into drinking and taking drugs. They have asked me if I want to come to their parties, and I have had to say no. I wish I could say it's because my mom would never let me... but that would be lying. I have to tell them that being around people getting drunk and high is not my idea of fun. They must think I am pretty weird. I feel like a freak around them.

Two of the three boys who have asked me out recently are both big-time drinkers, and the other one loves drugs. I am such a loser magnet! Where are the nice guys?

I am so glad that I get to babysit a lot. It means I can give a lot of "I'm busy" answers to these guys... and I am not even lying.

Love, Donna

> Donna said she thought people at church were perfect. Do you think that is really true? What are things that all people have in common?

❖ ❖

Dear Jesus,

I know it's been a while since I wrote to You. School is okay. My marks are still not very good. I feel so dumb most of the time. I do well in gym, but even my marks in gym are bad. I wish we got marks for lunch and spares.

It was a rough evening for me. Elly's dad, Mr. Fisher, and I had a bit of a fight. My dad phoned while I was at their place. I knew he was drunk. Elly and I were listening to music and just hanging out. Mr. Fisher said Dad wanted to come up for a visit. I told him that he was drunk and that it wasn't the best time to visit with him. Mr. Fisher knew my dad embarrassed me. He told me I should never be embarrassed about my dad. It didn't change anything. I was still embarrassed. Dad did behave himself. I am glad about that. He wanted Mr. Fisher to help him get a job as a security officer.

Love, Donna

❖ ❖

Dear Jesus,

Why is there so much dying around me?

Last night, Sandra died. You must have seen the whole thing. She was babysitting and high on drugs. She needed cigarettes and ran onto the road right in front of a truck. She died instantly.

We saw the crowd of people, and that was enough. Why do people want a close-up view of terrible things?

I feel sorry for her mom and dad. She was an only child. She was always so mean to them. Her parents gave her lots of clothes and stuff. Sandra used to swear at her mom. I felt sorry for her mom. I knew Sandra since grade one. She was mad at people a lot. I was never one of her favourites, because I was not very popular.

I find it very hard to believe that I will never see Sandra again. What happens to people like her when they die and their life is such a mess?

Love, Donna

Is death something that you are afraid of? How can Jesus comfort you when you think about death?

❖ ❖

Dear Jesus,

Today, Elly and I sat at the funeral home all day. Sandra's mom asked Elly and me to sit with her. So we did. She told us that if her daughter had been better friends with us, then maybe she wouldn't be dead.

I felt guilty, but the truth is, I didn't like hanging out with Sandra. I never felt safe with her and she didn't like doing the same stuff I did.

It was a very sad day. Her parents' hearts are broken.

Jesus, what do you do with broken hearts?

Love, Donna

P.S. Mr. Fisher helped Dad get a job today. Now he is a security officer. He really likes it.

Have you ever had to spend a day somewhere to be a help to someone, and it really was not much fun? What happened?

❖ ❖

Dear Jesus,

Grade ten is good. My marks are still bad. But I guess You know that. I decided to go back to church again. I missed the people there. I really like the youth group.

Jesus, it was really neat getting baptized. I really liked telling everyone about how You and I got to be such good friends. I loved the feeling that I was doing something that made You smile at me.

My family didn't come. Everyone else had their parents and even grandparents there. I had my youth group and some of their parents. That was nice, but not the same as my family.

I wish they came.

Love, Donna

> *Have you ever wanted family to come to something special, but they didn't? How did you feel about that?*

❖ ❖

Dear Jesus.

Today was another scary day in my life. I feel very mixed up about adults.

Sara is a really good friend of Vandy's and mine. I always knew her father was a bit crazy, and an alcoholic, but I didn't know he was completely nuts.

Sara's father set their apartment on fire and then shot their poor cat dead. Then he went looking for

Sara! Oh, thank goodness he didn't find her. Vandy and I hid her in our apartment and locked the door. We were terrified he would come. Finally, the police came. They took him away and then Sara went and stayed with her aunt far away.

Thank You for keeping us safe, Jesus. I was sad to see Sara leave. I don't think we will ever see her again.

Life is so hard sometimes. I really don't understand what would make a dad do all that Sara's dad did. Suddenly my dad is not looking so bad.

I feel nothing inside right now, Jesus. Maybe it has just been too scary a day for me.

Thank You for giving me courage.

Love, Donna

❖ ❖

Dear Jesus,

I was talking to some kids at school today and the subject quickly turned to God and all the kids and me were asking, "Does God really exist?" I know You heard the whole conversation.

There are some things I don't get about this world. Like, why do people think You and Your Father don't exist because they don't believe in You?

Today, talking to those kids, I felt like they think faith is for losers. Like, there is no way to be "in the cool club" and follow You at the same time. It's like they were saying, "Faith is for the weak." Well, Jesus, I guess I am weak then. I don't want to walk one more day without You. Life is just too hard. I need You to help me make sense of it all.

I was really mad when they moved on to the acceptable swearing conversation. They were talking about how it is not okay to say the "f" word, but it's okay to say Your name, Jesus, or Your Father's name, whenever they are mad, surprised or whatever.

For people who don't know You yet, they certainly mention Your name a lot. You get blamed for a lot of stuff, Jesus. I wonder sometimes, what do You think about all of this? I think it is dumb. I told them that maybe they should think about what they were saying.

I hope they heard some of what I said, anyway. I was pretty mad. I think a loving approach might have been better. Hopefully, next time.

Love, Donna

> *How would you respond if asked,*
> *"Does God really exist?"*

❖ ❖

Dear Jesus,

Yesterday was a day I don't think I'll ever forget. Elly, a few other girlfriends and I spent the day at a Christian camp. We wore matching blouses—I've never done that before. It was lots of fun. Everything was going smoothly until after supper.

We were all playing on the swings at the park. (I know that sounds a little immature for 16-year-old girls, but we were not out to impress anyone.) I needed to go to the ladies room.

When I went in, some girls were there, which is to be expected. I went into one of the stalls and did as one is supposed to do. I had just gotten myself down to business when the girls started screaming at the top of their lungs, because there was a bat flying around in the bathroom!

They called out to their big, hero boyfriends to rescue them. They bravely ran in with brooms and tried to hit the bat. All of this happened while I was trying to finish what I'd started.

All of a sudden, the bat flew over my stall and into my hair. I am pretty sure I wrecked the old saying that bats never fly into a woman's hair! It was quite a panic as I tried to get my pants up and get the bat out of my hair all at the same time. Meanwhile, the guys almost broke the stall door down to try to help me.

Finally, I got the bat out of my hair without it biting me, thankfully. It was the one time I wished I had short hair instead of long, curly hair. I was terrified the thing would bite me!

I know You see everything. I wonder how many people in the whole earth have ever had a bat stuck in their hair in the bathroom?

One thing I know for sure, I am unique.

Thank You for a lot of fun and for keeping me safe.

Love, Donna

❖ ❖

Dear Jesus,

High school is so frustrating. All around me there are girls who sleep with their boyfriends. They keep treating me like a "weirdo" just because I don't want to do that. Why would I? Forgive me, but I think the whole thing sounds kind of gross. Maybe one day I will change my mind, but I am not ready to today.

Besides, Jesus, where is the guy for me? The only boys who have asked me out are drug dealers and potheads. Why would I give myself to them? I would have to have "idiot" tattooed to my head!

I don't know what to say to them all. I honestly don't even like kissing, let alone all the rest of that stuff. Am I really weird, Jesus?

I also don't understand why having a boyfriend is so cool. It looks like it would be nice, but then I would need one I actually liked. That hasn't happened yet.

Well, Jesus, I want You to know what I have been thinking about. I do like some boys at my youth group, but I don't think they've noticed me. There is one who does, but even if he was the last guy on the planet, I would still choose to be single. He even told me if he wasn't dating another girl, he would be dating me!

Am I supposed to feel happy about that? I am so glad he is dating the other girl. She is welcome to him.

One day, I think I will meet the right guy. It sure isn't today.

Love, Donna

> *What are the qualities of the kind of person that you would like to date?*

❖ ❖

Dear Jesus,

Today, I helped Mom at her centre. It is an outpatient program. I love how she works with the people. They sure have their troubles. Some are schizophrenics, some alcoholics, while others are drug addicts, all trying to get better.

Today was a big lesson day for me. When I went to Mom's centre, Florence was there. I really like Florence. She is a very sweet, wrinkled-up woman. Mom says she had a terrible childhood. I found out that Florence thinks I am her best friend. That was really nice until she asked me to give her a kiss on her cheek. Jesus, I just didn't want to. Florence drools and I just find that gross.

When I didn't kiss Florence, Mom looked angry and told me to follow her, so I did. I will never forget her words: "Don't you ever come and tell me about Jesus and all that stuff until you can love people the way He did."

I felt like I got hit over the head. I know I hurt Florence's feelings. Please forgive me. Help me to see people like you do. I know You want me to love all people, even the Florences.

I want to tell my family about You, but it is very hard. I seem to blow it all the time, especially with my mom.

I never realized how much harder it is to live what You believe to be true than to talk about it.

Jesus, please help me live the way I should.

Love, Donna

❖ ❖

Dear Jesus,

I am wondering what to do with my life after I finish high school. I am thinking about becoming a social worker or a probation officer. I just don't know what I should do. Mom says I can do anything I put my mind to. I find it incredible she says that when my marks are so pathetic. Jesus, I want You to know I am not failing, though.

Love, Donna

What do you want to do when you are finished school?

❖ ❖

Dear Jesus,

I guess I always knew that the day would come when my dad would have to leave us forever.

Today was that day.

Our evening at home was going so well. Vandy, Doug, and I were all at home doing different stuff. Doug was working on something in his room. He had built a cool lock for his door and put it on earlier in the week, and Mom and Dad both knew about it.

The moment Dad walked through the front door, I knew he was not only drunk, but very angry. I also knew it had nothing to do with us, because we hadn't seen him all day. He stormed down the hall toward Doug's room with a hammer in his hand. He tore the lock from the door and threw the hammer at Doug's head. It came so close to hitting him—You must have been watching over him, Jesus. I could not believe it. The hammer missed his head, but flew into the screen window and just dangled there. It could have gone through and killed someone on the street below. Just as Dad threw the hammer, my mom came home and started screaming at Dad.

Vandy started crying and ran to her room. Doug went and sat in his closet and shut the door. Then Dad grabbed Mom and slammed her against the wall. I got really, really mad. I know You saw me, Jesus.

Somehow, I got in between them and pinned my dad to the wall. I told him it was time for him to leave. I got a garbage bag, put his clothes in and threw the bag outside the door in the hall. Then I told him to leave or I'd call the police.

He left.

I think he knew I meant it.

By this time, everyone was crying but me. I was just plain mad.

I felt so bad for my brother. He sat in his closet for a long time. The cat went in and sat with him. In our house, it seems our cat is often the most comfort we can find. At least he wasn't alone. Jesus, I am so thankful to have You to talk to. Mom was glad Dad left.

She thanked me later.

Thank You for giving me the courage to do what I did tonight, God. I don't know where Dad is going to go, but right now, I honestly don't care. I am pretty sure you understand my feelings, Jesus.

Love, Donna

Can you relate to this story? When was a time that Jesus gave you courage?

❖ ❖

Dear Jesus,

I cannot believe my history teacher wrote the word "Bible" on the blackboard and then proceeded to put a big "X" through it.

When I asked him why, he said, "The Bible is totally unreliable." I put my hand up again and asked him when he had read it.

"Never," he answered.

So I said, "How do you know anything about something you've never read?"

To which he replied, "Everyone knows the Bible is full of contradictions."

I said, "Name one." He couldn't.

Then I told him to take the "X" off the word Bible written on the blackboard. He did. He was red. I was redder. I was so mad, Jesus.

The kids in class didn't mock me or anything.

I can't believe how much people don't like You, Jesus—You or Your word, it seems.

I like reading my Bible. I love the Psalms. Psalm 91 and 121 are my current favourites.

Love, Donna

❖ ❖

Dear Jesus,

Today, I thought I was going to die. When Elly and I went to Herb and Vicki's, our neighbors. I could tell Herb had been drinking. I am used to that, so it didn't bother me. When we went on the balcony though, Elly, Herb and I started to horse around, and suddenly Herb grabbed me from behind and held me by my feet over the balcony.

Jesus, I know You heard my prayer. The tenth floor balcony is very high. It scares me all over again just writing this to You, Jesus.

Thank You for keeping me safe from the crazy people who seem to live all around me. I cannot believe all the things that happen.

Jesus, I am so sad watching so many of our friends as they get into drugs and drinking. I just don't understand how it is fun. When I see the booze, I think of how it ruined my family. When I see the drugs, I think of the people at Mom's centre and the path drugs and alcohol led them down.

Jesus, I don't want to walk on that path. I have to tell You, Jesus, life would be way too scary without You. I'm going to continue to walk with you on your path.

Love, Donna

Donna talks about how happy she is to have Jesus in her life and how He has helped her. What does it mean to follow on Jesus' path?

❖ ❖

_____

_____

_____

_____

_____

_____

_____

_____

_____

_____

_____

_____

_____

_____

_____

_____

_____

_____

_____

_____

_____

_____

_____

_____

_____

_____

_____

_____

Chapter 7

Decisions, Decisions—
What is a Girl to Do?

Dear Jesus,

I am thinking about maybe going to Bible College. I have been talking to some of the college and career young people at my church, who are already going. They seem to really like it. I have no idea what you do at Bible College. I guess I would learn a lot about You and the Bible.

We both know I have a lot to learn.

I mentioned it to Mom. She didn't seem exactly taken with the idea. No one from my mom or dad's side has ever gone to Bible College.

I want to go far away to college. I am tired of all the crazy stuff around me. I would never be able to think about what I am learning if I stayed nearby. I need a break!

Dad's basement apartment is nearby. I know he is doing better than I have ever seen him before. Who will take care of him if I am not here? Jesus, I would need You to take care of him. There is no one else to ask. It would be easier if he didn't live alone. I know that Vandy or Doug would check on him, but I need someone who would take care of him every day. You are the only one who is up for it, Jesus. I am pretty sure You would do a way better job than me. It is too much for me. I know that now. I guess I didn't realize how hard it has been. Jesus, please take care of him if I go?

Love, Donna

❖ ❖

Dear Jesus,

I was so excited on Sunday when one of my church friend's whole family took Elly and I out to a restaurant after church. The whole restaurant was filled with church families. I guess that is what people do after service. It was really nice for them to invite us. I had chicken.

Love, Donna

❖ ❖

Dear Jesus,

My family is not impressed with the idea of me going to Bible College. I don't know what I would do with a Bible College degree, but I would like to work with kids who come from a home like mine. I have no idea how to make that happen. I'll just trust You.

I do feel excited about the possibility of leaving home. Show me where to go, Jesus.

Help me find a good job this summer. Mom can't help me at all with the cost of college. I will apply for a student loan and go from there.

Love, Donna

> *Have you asked God for direction for your future? What do you sense God wants you to do?*

❖ ❖

Dear Jesus,

Thank You for a really amazing day. I don't mind being a waitress, especially today when Dad walked in and ordered a coffee. He must have thought I did pretty well, because when he left he gave me a $100 tip for my college courses! He said he had another $400 for college, too. He wants to give it to me to help. He must not be feeling too upset about my plans. That is so neat. Mom is not too thrilled.

Baseball season is going really well. My team wins pretty well every week. I think the other teams are going to hate us soon. I have to admit to you that I like winning.

I am busy getting ready for my friend Debbie's wedding. I have never been in a wedding before. It is so cool that she even asked me. It will be a lot of fun. I can't really imagine getting married right now. I have a lot I am hoping to do first.

Anyway, thanks for a really neat day.

Love, Donna

> *If you were going to describe your skills and talents, what would you say?*

❖ ❖

Dear Jesus,

I don't understand people. I'm sure You have to because You made them. There was a guy on the subway, and we were talking about all kinds of stuff. When I asked him what he thought about You, Jesus, he told me that "he didn't give a @#*@!" Wow, I have never heard anyone say that before. Maybe they might say "not too interested right now," but that was certainly blunt. I told him he may want to rethink that if he finds himself dead one day... which he will one day, because we all will.

Still shocked.

Love, Donna

❖ ❖

Dear Jesus,

Thanks for my job. Thanks, too, for Danny. He is the cutest guy in my French class. He really is the reason I took the class in the first place. He sat behind me every class. I told him about You quite a bit. Not as much as he claims, though! I was amazed when he told me he asked You to be his Saviour. He said all my bugging him to give his life to You got to him. He says his mom is a Christian and he couldn't handle us both bugging him. I had no idea that his mom was a Christian. Maybe it was because of all his mom's prayers that I gave him such a hard time in French class.

I know You answer prayers. Thank You that You never let me down. Stuff in life doesn't always turn out exactly as I was praying, but it turns out for the better. Thank You, Jesus. Thanks for helping my mom accept my going away to Bible College. I really want to go, Jesus.

I can't wait.

Love, Donna

What are some of the prayers that God has answered for you?

❖ ❖

_____

_____

_____

_____

_____

_____

_____

Chapter 8

"Go West, Young Woman"

Dear Jesus,

Mom seemed mad when she and Dad took me to the train. I really don't think Mom was so much mad as she was sad. At least, that is my theory. At the train station she said it was the same platform she left from when she was 18. She left home when she was the same age as me. I never knew that.

I can't believe I am on the train heading for Bible College. You have to wonder who goes to Bible College... are they all freaks?

I can't believe how flat the prairies are. Wow!

I love the trees and passing by Lake Superior. It is the biggest lake I have ever seen!

Jesus, come with me as I meet all these people. I am definitely worried.

I am thankful there are a few people from my church who will be there. I know they won't want me hanging out with them too much. I am younger than them, so they might just think I am in the way. I don't want that. Jesus, help me make friends quickly so I don't get in their way.

Help me see the people like You do.

Love, Donna

❖ ❖

Dear Jesus,

Bible College is great. There are lots of nice people, although some are weird. I feel like a bit of a loser here, Jesus. All of these people come from beautiful families—at least it seems like they do, and they all sure know their Bibles. It seems they know every Bible story from the whole Bible. On the quiz there was one question, "What is circumcision?" At least I knew the right answer. I was proud of myself. One guy thought it was a type of food. That was comforting.

At least I know You, Jesus. I know You are faithful and I'm here for a reason, and You have a plan for my life.

Thank You for my very nice roommate, Karen. I find her very warm and friendly. She is a Mennonite. I thought Mennonites all rode horses and lived on farms with no electricity. Not here! They are nice people—pretty normal really. I don't understand why they all sing so well. Is that part of being Mennonite? I have never been in a place where it seems every girl sings and plays the piano (in case singing wasn't enough). Well, I hope that isn't a prerequisite for being here, because I don't think I will be doing either of those things anytime soon. I am good at having fun and making people laugh. I hope that counts for something!

Love, Donna

> *Have you ever felt you were different from anyone else?*

❖ ❖

Dear Jesus,

The people who go to Bible College all seem super smart. I got my marks for systematic theology today and I can't believe that I got 62%! I couldn't believe I got that high a mark. They were all feeling badly for me. I was thrilled! That is a great mark. I passed by quite a bit even.

I find this class completely irrelevant. What difference does this make in my life? How is this supposed to help someone live a life that is pleasing to You?

There are some smart guys in my class who absolutely love it, though. Two in particular who both want to teach full-time. They know that this stuff makes no sense to me, so they've decided to practice on me. They think if they can teach me, they can teach anyone.

Well, I will let them find out how gifted they are at teaching. Between You and me, I am not going to make it easy for them. I think that would be more helpful for them.

I promise I will try to be nice.

Love, Donna

❖ ❖

Dear Jesus,

I was so surprised to get a phone call from Doug today. Usually it's Mom who phones on a Sunday. I had been praying for him all weekend. I couldn't get him off my mind. When he called, he said he knew that I must have been praying, because he had been in a car accident. He had been driving with a bunch of friends. He lost control of the car and crashed. The police told him they were very lucky. Doug said he knew they weren't lucky, but that I was praying for them and God kept them safe.

That was so cool, Jesus. Your Spirit tells us to pray for very good reason. Thank You for keeping Doug and his friends safe.

Love, Donna

> Can you remember a time you prayed for someone because they came to mind, and you felt you should?

❖ ❖

Dear Jesus,

I can't believe I'm on the social committee. We get to plan all the fun stuff. Finally I get to do something I am really good at.

The administration of the school said my marks should be higher and maybe I should drop the social committee. I told them my marks wouldn't be any higher if I wasn't on the committee. They let me stay. Thank You, Jesus, for helping me.

There are a lot of rules here. I find it strange to have a curfew. I have never had one in my life before. In fact, I had never even heard of a curfew. The Dean of Women said that I am oblivious to rules. I told her I was sorry, but to be honest I didn't know what "oblivious" meant. She told me I needed to look it up.

Love, Donna

❖ ❖

Dear Jesus,

Today I received a letter from my Uncle Doug, my dad's only brother. I never see him, but he wrote to tell me that I am "wasting my money and my life at Bible College."

I honestly don't care what Uncle Doug thinks. I know that I am exactly where I am supposed to be. I do care what my dad thinks, though. Last night I dreamt my dad died. I think maybe I should write a letter to him, because I really want him to know why I don't think I am wasting my life, and why I want to live the rest of my life the way You want me to.

Jesus, I know You see my heart. I have prayed for my dad since I was twelve years old. Please don't let him die before he makes peace with You, Jesus. I pray that he would know what it means to be forgiven and loved by the One who created him. Whisper into his ear, Jesus, your love for him. Help him to know that none of us have ever done anything too horrible for you not to forgive them.

I know You heal people from the inside, Jesus. I know You are healing me. Thank You. I wish with all of my heart I could make my dad know how much You love him.

Help me write a very good letter.

Love, Donna

> *Donna talks about Jesus healing her heart. What do you think she means? Has Jesus ever healed your heart? If so, how?*

❖ ❖

Dear Jesus,

Last night was probably the best prank my friend and I have ever pulled. I don't really feel safe writing it all out in detail, because who knows who might read this! All I can say is there are some guys in the men's dorm who may notice significant changes. Don't worry—we were the only ones around. I think this type of thing is one of my most favourite activities. The poor Dean of Women is probably praying for me. That is okay. I like it when people pray for me.

Love, Donna

❖ ❖

Dear Jesus,

When the Dean of Women called my friend and me into her office, I thought little of it. I have gotten into so much trouble these last few months.

I find it hard to remember all the rules. I honestly thought she had found out what we did the night before. I could not have been farther from the truth.

When she said my mom was waiting for me to phone home and that I needed to prepare myself for some bad news, I was scared. How exactly does a person prepare for bad news? I asked Mrs. Marco to pray for me, and then I phoned.

The news was horrible. My dad suffered a massive heart attack and died that morning. He was in his car on his way to work. They found his car pulled over to the side of the highway and he had already passed away. Mom said in his coat pocket was the letter I had just written him. It was opened.

I was devastated by the news of my dad. I went back to my room and just cried my heart out... I am sure You were with me, Jesus. I was so sad I thought my heart would break in two.

Mom said there was an airline ticket waiting for me at the airport. I only had a few hours before my plane would be leaving. As I write this, I just can't believe it. I am in shock sitting on this plane flying home. When I got on the plane, the flight attendant asked me if she could help me because I was crying and not eating anything. I told her I was on my way to my dad's funeral. She left for a minute and then came back and asked me to come and sit in first class. That was very nice of her.

Psalm 46 was my prayer, Jesus. No matter how bad life gets, I know that You are still with me. Please help me, Jesus. I find this so hard to believe. I really thought I would see Dad go to church and put his faith in You, Jesus.

I am so thankful You led me to write the letter to him. I know I told him how much You love him no matter what he had done wrong. Jesus, I give him to You again. I leave him in Your care, and even though I am really confused right now, I believe that You know exactly what You are doing. I need to trust You. Soothe my aching heart, Lord. Walk with me, Jesus. The valley is very dark.

Love, Donna

Do you see God's hand in Donna's story?
How is he working in her life?

❖ ❖

Dear Jesus,

Thank You for helping me through this last week. I feel numb and like I'm going to break into pieces, but thanks for helping me through Dad's funeral. Jesus, I cannot believe how much strength and peace I had. It was very strange. I should have been falling apart, but I felt a deep calmness in my heart, so much so that many people commented. I honestly didn't know what to say, except that it must be what it feels like to have a lot of people praying for you. I certainly noticed.

In Your Word, it says that You will give to me a peace that passes all understanding. You have done that. Thank You.

Now I am supposed to study for exams, but my brain can't seem to think. Please help me, Jesus. I really don't care too much about exams, even though I know I should.

I feel lost. Help me to get through these exams one at a time. I just need some energy here!

Please help! Donna

❖ ❖

Dear Jesus,

I find studying really hard. I have very little energy to do anything. I can't concentrate. I keep wondering about my dad. Is he in heaven? I know he was still drinking at the end, though I am positive he was sober when he died. I feel bad that he was alone.

I am amazed that no one was killed. It can't be every day someone has a heart attack while driving.

I don't understand why You allowed him to die. I didn't get to say goodbye, but I'm thankful that You warned me in my dream, and I was able to write that letter to him. I am so thankful that at least he got my letter and read it, and I was able to tell him how much You love him, Jesus.

I know You are full of grace. Even as You were dying on the cross, You told the thief on the cross next to You that he would be with You in paradise that very day. I am pretty sure that the thief didn't go to church, get baptized or even pray.

I wish I had the power to make people know that You are real and that You see everything. Not that life becomes perfect, but it sure is different with You.

I ask You to give my heart peace, Jesus. It is so hard to study, and I have to write exams in a few days.

Thank You, Donna

Have you ever grieved the loss of someone? What comfort can faith in Jesus bring?

❖ ❖

Dear Jesus,

I survived exams. I think I got the highest marks I have ever received. Not as high as other people, but amazing for me! I am glad this year is over. I have had enough of Bible College for one year. I love the people, though. Everyone is so different. I have made a lot of good friends, and found people accepted me pretty much for who I am.

I still feel kind of numb, Jesus. I can't believe that when I go back home, my dad won't be there. That makes me very sad.

I need You to walk beside me, Jesus.

Thanks... Donna

❖ ❖

Dear Jesus,

Thanks for the people you sent to help me study. I know I did better than I would have if I was alone.

It has been good getting to know so many different people at college. They are certainly lots of fun, and then there are the weird ones. I guess they are everywhere. I tried to get to know some of them a bit. I am not sure I will ever figure them out. They do keep the world interesting, though.

When I get home, please help me get a decent job. Lead me. I have no idea where to start looking.

Some of my friends say there are some cute boys at home waiting to take me out. That is really nice. I find it hard to believe, but I'll have fun.

Help me to live my life so that my family sees You. Home is the hardest place to live the way You want me to.

I sure need Your help.

Love, Donna

❖ ❖

_____

_____

_____

_____

_____

_____

_____

_____

_____

_____

_____

_____

_____

Chapter 9

Summer Relief in So Many Ways

Dear Jesus,

It is nice to be home. My mom was very happy to see me. She even asked me if I wanted a cup of tea. I know it doesn't sound like much, but it was huge for me. Mom told me to go and sit on the balcony and she would make it and bring it to me. In my 19 years of living, this was history in the making! It was very nice. I felt special. Mom sat down beside me and listened to me go on and on about Bible College, and all my friends and our many adventures. I wish my dad was here, though. I would have loved to tell him all my stories too. It is so hard to believe he is really gone forever. I feel this constant pain in my heart. I hope it goes away one day.

Mom laughed a lot, though. I think she was surprised that Bible College students can do so many crazy things. If she met these people she would understand. They are pretty unique. It is hard to believe some of them are thinking of being ministers.

They will be very different from any minister I know. I guess they will have to change a bit or no one will listen to them!

Thanks for pointing out the Red Cross job to me. I think I can do that. The lady who hired me seems really nice. It's not hard caring for people.

There are lots of weddings this summer.

I wonder if I will ever get married. I find that pretty hard to believe right now. When I think of the guys I know, I can't believe any of them would want me... and to be honest, I am not so sure I would want them. Think of all the nice, perfect predictable kind of girls they could choose. I am not predictable. The guys I know want piano-playing, singing girls... we both know, that ain't me. It seems to be a big deal to the guys who want to be pastors. I think it would be kind of cool to be a pastor's wife, but honestly, I don't feel like I am exactly pastor's wife material.

I do want a guy from a somewhat healthy family, though. It is too much work if we are both screwed up... truth be told.

Help me in this job, Lord. I know I ask it all the time, but please help me to love people the way You do. I can't do that alone.

Love, Donna

Do you ever wonder if you will find a life partner? Could you write a prayer about this?

❖ ❖

Dear Jesus,

I love when my mom and I have really good heart-to-heart talks. A few nights ago, she told me about her mom and explained why she seemed so cold all the time. She told me that Grandma only told my mom once in her entire life that she loved her. Apparently, Grandma lost many of her dearest friends in the First World War. She also told me the story of how brokenhearted my grandma was when her six-year-old daughter died of pneumonia. She thought Grandma never got over losing her. It doesn't make the things Grandma said about my dad right, or excuse her for being mean, but it does help me understand a little more of her journey.

It is sad, though, Jesus, how my mom also finds it difficult to tell us she loves us. She never shows us any affection. I hope when I'm a mom one day, or Vandy is a mom, that we don't continue in the same way with our kids. It needs to end somewhere.

The talk with Mom helps me to forgive Grandma. I know, Jesus, You have wanted me to forgive my grandma for a long time now. So, Jesus, I do forgive her for the mean things she said about my dad and the hurtful things she said to me over the years. I will let her go. Heal those memories, Jesus.

Thank You.

Love, Donna

Can you write about someone you need to forgive who has hurt you?

❖ ❖

_____

_____

_____

_____

_____

_____

_____

_____

_____

_____

_____

_____

_____

_____

_____

_____

_____

_____

_____

_____

_____

_____

_____

_____

_____

Chapter 10

Another Year of College

Dear Jesus,

It is great to see my friends at college again. I had a wonderful summer back home, but I'm glad to be back. It was hard saying goodbye to my mom. We had a lot of good talks.

I am just wondering what I am going to do after I finish Bible College. I know I have two years to get through, but I would just like to know what I'm preparing for.

I have to mention to You that I did notice a boy. Unfortunately, he is a Mennonite and his dad is a pastor—probably a little too perfect for me. I don't like his name, either. I can't imagine having to call someone that for the rest of my life. Why would someone name their kid that? From now on, I will call him Bartholomew, Bart for short because it is easier to spell. Just between You and me, okay?

I found out there are a few other people here who come from an alcoholic family. It is nice to know there are people who understand. I know their stories are different. I have watched them. They don't stand out. It is funny because sometimes I feel like I glow in the dark because I am so different. It is probably only what I feel, rather than what people actually believe about me.

I have to keep reminding myself that I am not a loser just because my dad was an alcoholic and he left us. I know that in my head, but I find it really tough to let it sink into my heart. Jesus, I really need You to look over my heart and to heal me. I don't think there is anyone else who can really heal all the rips and tears like You.

Thank You for helping me each day. You are my faithful friend, Jesus.

Love, Donna

What lies have you been telling yourself (about you), that you need to stop believing?

❖ ❖

Dear Jesus,

Well, I had a really good day today, but it sure ended strangely. I was at a conference and I spent the whole day with an amazing guy from seminary. I wouldn't dream of him noticing me in any way, except to think that I am funny. I think he's great.

One of the girls from my dorm must have watched us as he walked me back to our dorm when the day was over. She told me later that I shouldn't think of that guy romantically, because he would never look at a girl like me. I felt hurt, Jesus. Even if I know in my heart that is true, she did not need to point it out. If she is interested in him, she has no need to feel worried because of me. I am not on the guy's radar. I am quite sure.

I think that one day, there will be someone who knows everything about me and will still choose me. I find that a little hard to believe at the moment, though, Jesus. I can believe it for everyone else around me, but not really for me.

Thank You for choosing me, Jesus. You have seen everything and You still love me. You accept me. I ask You to help me to forgive this girl for being unkind. Jesus, I ask that You would heal my heart.

It hurts a lot today.

Love, Donna

❖ ❖

Dear Jesus,

I thought that I would die laughing today. Remember Bart? (He is the guy with the not-so-great name I told You about.) Well, we saw Bart stumble over the fence into the snow... that was funny. I guess we scared him pretty badly on the way to serve breakfast. Lucky for him it was still real snowy and dark. Maybe it would have been even more embarrassing had it happened in daylight.

I can't believe the pranks girls in my dorm like to pull. I was one of the few they were trying to freak out. I knew they were up to something. They were acting too weird. I think they may get into some serious trouble for pulling the fire alarm and running all over the girls' dorm like a bunch of lunatics. I tried to look surprised because they worked so hard.

Today, I found out I actually have to take singing lessons in order to graduate!! That is horrible! I told them that is not what I do. They said I could either take piano lessons or voice. I couldn't believe it, so I chose singing. I am even supposed to do a recital. I am speechless! I can think of many things I would rather do than learn to sing or play piano! I'd rather clean bathrooms for a credit if they made that an option. We could call it the servant class.

Love, Donna

❖ ❖

Dear Jesus,

I know I haven't written a lot to You this year at school. It has been going well for the most part. I am still on the social committee. I wish they could give me marks for doing that. Then I would possibly get my first "A."

This year at college, we were each asked to go and help out somewhere. I found this really neat group home nearby. The kids are pretty rough. It sure doesn't take brain surgery to know that life has not treated them kindly. I love going each week and playing games or just hanging out with them. It just feels right to me to be with these kids. I can understand them, Lord, and my heart aches for what they have gone through and are still going through in their hearts.

About the friendship with the Mennonite guy "Bart," well, the romance is going nowhere. He's made it pretty clear that while he thinks I'm a nice girl, he also said, "You are a pretty scary choice." At least that is how I interpret our last conversation.

I heard there is a nice girl from a nice Mennonite family interested in him. I even met her. I didn't dare ask her if she sang and played the piano. I think I would have thrown up if she said yes. She has that yes-I-play-and-sing look. She probably bakes and sews, too... seems pretty much perfect—so I don't think there is much I can do except leave this with You.

I sure feel lousy. It is hard to let go of him. I really thought he was the guy You chose for me.

Donna

❖ ❖

Dear Jesus,

It is great to be home again. I can't believe how fast time goes in college.

I really love my new summer job at Youth Unlimited.

The staff is amazing! I can't believe I get paid to love and care for kids, not to mention all the games we play. I am not sure who has more fun—the kids or me. Thank You, Jesus, for the privilege I know is mine.

Please use me this summer to touch the hearts and lives of some of these kids, Lord. I'm so glad You led me to this place.

Love, Donna

❖ ❖

Dear Jesus,

I am going to go broke paying for dresses to be in these summer weddings!

I never think about that part when people ask me to stand with them. I have to get used to the makeup thing, though. We have to wear tons of the stuff and I'm not into makeup. The mascara weighs my eyelids down and makes blinking feel like exercise. I feel like my lips glow in the dark.

This summer is going pretty fast, Lord. I love the late Friday night games of cards with my mom and Vandy. That is a lot of fun.

Love, Donna

❖ ❖

Dear Jesus,

I have decided that weddings are a lot of work. Not to mention stressful. There are eight million details to remember. At least I only had to try to look decent in the photos. That was stressful. I am no model, that is for sure. Truthfully, it was a lot of fun being in those weddings. You have given me a lot of really great friends. It has been good hanging out with all these people.

I find it hard to believe that I am going to have to make a decision about what I am going to do after college. It has gone by soooo fast. I am thinking about volunteering at Youth Unlimited in Winnipeg while I am at college. That would be fun. Well... I will wait and see.

Love, Donna

❖ ❖

Chapter 11

The Final College Year

Dear Jesus,

Thank You for an amazing summer. It was so neat to see those kids respond to the message that You make a big difference in life. Watching them give their lives to You thrilled my heart more than anything I have ever experienced before.

I can't believe this is my last year here at Bible College. I pray that You will teach me the things I need to learn. I know I am not the best at writing papers. It never matters how long I spend writing the dumb things, I get the same low marks—that's not very encouraging. Maybe my mother is right, I am dyslexic and it does affect my ability to communicate my thoughts in writing. I wish I could write as well as I speak.

I am also thinking it is unfortunate I got kicked out of typing in grade nine. I don't know if I ever mentioned that to You. I really disliked it. So, one day I was playing with my bag of carrots at the back of class. I was practicing a highly effective flinging technique. The problem was, I accidentally launched it, and well let's just say the teacher got it right in the middle of her forehead. I didn't mean to be disrespectful, though I have to say, I wasn't so sad when it happened. Now I regret it because I have to pay someone to type all my papers. That is expensive.

You probably noticed that I still have my eye on that Mennonite guy, Bart. I am a very stubborn girl. I should probably give up... but liking him does keep life interesting. There is nothing I can do to change where I come from. I can't apologize for the family You put me in. Who knows? Maybe he will get over it.

I really like preaching class. I actually get great marks in that class. It feels strange to be the only girl. The guys are quick to remind me I am female. Thank goodness I have them to remind me of my gender.

Jesus, I trust in the days to come that You will use me in significant ways to further your kingdom... even if I am a girl, or a woman... whatever I am. "Woman" seems too mature to me.

Love, Donna

You may notice that Donna is allowing her past to determine who she is. Do you ever do the same thing?

❖ ❖

Dear Jesus,

This weekend a traveling evangelist came to my Bible College. He spoke at a number of services. On one of the breaks, he approached me and a couple of my male buddies and asked us "guys" if we were going to be evangelists when we graduated. I guess he didn't realize that I was female (once again, I think my short haircut is doing me no favours!). The guys pointed at me and told him that he should ask me, since they thought evangelism was more up my alley than theirs.

He turned to me and asked me the same question again. I told him I would love to, especially since I love to share my faith with others. He became pretty uncomfortable when he realized I was a woman, and he mumbled something before walking away. The weird thing is he asked me the very same thing again the next day. I told him that I was still female and that seemed to be a problem for him. He apologized for bothering me and went on his way.

I feel so frustrated, Jesus, that You made me this way—I am not like other women who sing and play the piano. The gifts You gave to me seem better suited for a pastor or an evangelist. Both seem to be out of reach for me because I am female. I have to trust You to work out all the details.

I will never stop sharing my faith—it's what I truly love to do.

Love, Donna

Dear Jesus,

I'd like to write out a poem that a friend wrote. She told me that I inspired her to write it. I was pretty amazed when she said that. I can't say anyone has ever said I inspired anything like a poem before.

Babbling Brook

Babbling brook run through the woods
Laughing, sparkling, free, alive,
Make me like that little brook
Bring your life to all around.
Stagnant waters, trapped and spoiled,
Foul and wasted, fast asleep.
Bringing death instead of life,
Losing life within itself.

Break its banks and let it escape
The tomb in which it lies asleep
Pour your cleansing water through...
Your life flow through it clean and pure.
Let its stagnant wealth become
Alive, instilling life in all.
In passing, let it touch and heal
The scars of death it left before.
In my life work freely now
Break the banks of fear in me.

Let me be a lively brook.
Your life flow through me clean and pure.

Marilyn Rempel

What does this poem say to you?

❖ ❖

Dear Jesus,

I have been thinking a lot about forgiveness lately. I know you are waiting for me to forgive my dad especially. I loved him very much, but I also know that he disappointed me and let me down many times. I am thankful for his kindnesses of recent years, but that doesn't erase the hurt from days gone by.

I know forgiving him is a big part of the healing of my own heart. I hear forgiveness is more for my own sake than his. It seems kind of backward if you ask me. My heart is weighed down these days and I am struggling to move forward. As much as I would like to not forgive him, I know I need to.

I would like to think of Dad without the pain rising up inside me. I am very tired of that. So, Jesus, I forgive Dad for not being there for me to take me to the doctor or to provide for us as he should have, for tearing our family apart, for giving away my accordion, for letting down my mother, for not being sober at Christmas, for embarrassing me in front of my friends, for choosing the bottle over us. I forgive him, Jesus.

Please look inside my heart, Jesus, and heal every open and bleeding wound you see there. Replace all these negative emotions with love and the courage to let Dad off the hook, not just for today, but always.

I do not want to grow old and bitter. I know You forgave me, Jesus, for all the rotten stuff I have ever done, and I want to forgive those people who have hurt and disappointed me.

I know I am not perfect and really have no right to judge others. By forgiving, I know it helps me also to let go of the resentment I have held for so long.

Jesus, I ask You to help me walk in this forgiveness and the healing I know You will bring.

Love, Donna

> *What kind of forgiveness is Donna talking about? Is there anyone you need to forgive? Can you write about this?*

❖ ❖

Dear Jesus,

Thank You, Jesus, for all the beautiful friends You have given me this last year. We laughed a lot and prayed and made all kinds of discoveries about faith. I am thankful for the teachers, too. I would be lying if I said I love sitting in those classes, but I do appreciate all they strive to teach me. I struggle to understand what I am supposed to do with some of this stuff I learned. I am clearly not a student. I also wish I could have stood at the back of the class. I think better on my feet. Some people are really good at sitting. I cannot say that is my gift!

I am thankful for the privilege of working as a volunteer for the same organization, Youth Unlimited, as last year.

Listening to those five girls pray to receive you as their Saviour was so neat, Jesus. I told the girls about You, and how we are good friends and the difference it makes having You at my side all the time. They wanted You to be by their side all the time, too. Jesus, I know their lives are really tough. I pray that they will give You first place in their lives. Show me how to teach them in simple but helpful ways how to walk with You.

When I finish here at school, Jesus, I think I will work at Youth Unlimited. Jesus, can we do it this way? If you give me a car for $100, I will work here. If you don't, then I will know I am supposed to go home and work for the same organization back home.

Help me finish off the year. I am honestly tired of hanging out with Christians all the time. I like hanging out with the people whose lives are messy. I am not saying I don't like or even love these people at college, but a little variety is always nice. I am sorry, Jesus. I know You love them all, but I think You understand where I am coming from. I can't imagine working at a Bible College as a career. It would be very hard to know Your power and the amazing way You bring lost people to Yourself. Please don't make me work with Christians all the time. I honestly don't think I could do it.

I better go. I have a lot of studying I have to do.

Love, Donna

> *What do you think you would love to do for God?*

❖ ❖

Dear Jesus,

I am thankful that You got me through the year, Lord.

I am pretty sure it's official—"Bart" is not interested in me. I give him over to You. I feel sad. He told me he is worried about me being raised basically by my mother, because he thinks that I would struggle with the whole submission thing. It was something like that, Jesus. I can't actually tell You what he said because it makes me too mad. I am sure You heard everything. He's right, though. I don't get the submission idea. I doubt I would be very good at it. On the positive side (thankfully there is one), he thinks he would spend his life in my limelight because I preach better than he does. If Your plans for his future do not include me, then I am OK with

that, even though it breaks my heart. Help me to let
him go.

Feeling crushed.

Love, Donna

> *Sometimes things don't go the way we
> had hoped and prayed. Can you write
> about a time this happened?*

❖ ❖

Dear Jesus,

My good friends, Beatrice and Beverly's dad took
me to a small town where there was this skinny, but
super strong, minister. He showed me a blue Comet,
automatic car. He told me he was selling it for $1,000. I
told him about the ministry I would be starting in a few
weeks and that I only had $100, and he said, "Okay."
Can You believe it? One minor problem: I think it would
have been better to get my driver's license first! I
forgot that detail. I am learning to drive quickly. I am
pretty sure You must be helping me learn. When you're
driving and dyslexic it gets tricky. I keep forgetting
which side of the road to drive on and which hand is
which. I am going to start wearing the ring my mom
and sister gave me for graduating from Bible College.
At least I would know which hand is which at a glance.

I will start at Youth Unlimited right after I
graduate. Thank You for making my choice so clear.

I'm glad my classes are done. I think my eyeballs have read all the books and my ears have listened to all the lectures they can handle for a while.

I ask You to lead me through the ministry ahead. I know that these kids come from very broken homes. But, Jesus, You remind me of a Shepherd who isn't afraid to go to the dark and messy places to find lost and wounded sheep. You found me, and I am deeply grateful.

Love, Donna

> *Miracles still happen today. Have you experienced one or heard about one? Can you write about it?*

❖ ❖

Dear Jesus,

It is great to have my mom here for my graduation. I loved introducing her to all my friends she has heard a million things about. I couldn't help but notice my classmates were having big celebrations with their families. My mom took one of my girlfriends and me out to dinner. It was really nice.

I was also happy my mom came because otherwise I would have been thrown in the shower for stealing some guy's underwear out of the men's dorm room. Here's the perfectly good explanation: I washed the underwear first and then I marinated them in all of the girls' leftover perfume. Those guys deserved it, though, Lord. They were really nasty to a lot of the girls. They always played mean pranks on them and someone needed to teach them a lesson. I know You say You pay back in Your way in Your time, but it seemed like a good idea then. Those boys need to buy new underwear now. I am trying to feel badly, but that isn't going so well (as You know).

Love, Donna

❖ ❖

_____

_____

_____

_____

_____

_____

_____

_____

_____

_____

_____

_____

_____

_____

_____

_____

_____

_____

_____

_____

_____

_____

_____

_____

_____

_____

_____

_____

_____

_____

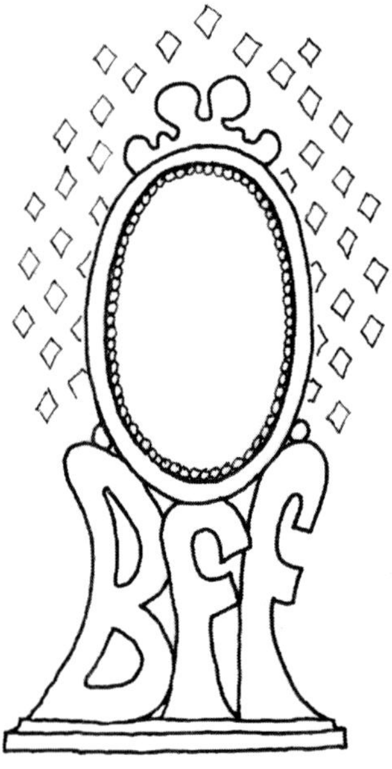
BFF

Chapter 12

Freedom Plus Adventure

Dear Jesus,

Well, graduation is over and now all I need is a cheap, safe place to live. I like my new job at YU. We have neat meetings and I love the clubs and all the girls. I really like the tough girls. I guess the challenge is kind of fun. There is quite a bit of training, though, to work with these kids. As part of the training, Beth (my amazing boss), I and a volunteer are going to take an outdoor wilderness training course. We are going to camp in the Rocky Mountains in Western Canada. I have never been there, Jesus. It will be so cool!

Wow, I do feel good about adventure, Jesus, and this work is full of adventure.

I am really enjoying my new church. The people are very nice and I have made some new friends there.

Jesus, please help me raise my support. I have never heard of having to raise your salary before. I really need Your help here. I am afraid to ask people. Yet, I know You want me here. My only choice is to write the letters asking for people to support me, and trust You that they won't mind.

I am heading back home to visit my mom. I know she is disappointed I am not moving back home. I know I am in the right place for now, though.

Love, Donna

> *Was there ever a time you had a need and you prayed and God provided?*

❖ ❖

Dear Jesus,

I think the drive to the outdoor training was the longest in my lifetime. I read the whole way. In fact, Beth even read to me as I drove, and then she got interested. So we read this massive book to each other as we took turns driving. It helped pass the time.

Jesus, when You and your Father made the mountains, You did a truly breathtaking job! I am struck by the majesty and beauty. I felt really small when I stood at the foot of those mountains. It sure is different seeing the mountains in person than just seeing pictures. Everything I have heard my whole life about the mountains is true. You really have the Creator thing down pat.

I don't know which part I liked the most—mountain climbing and rappelling or hiking. I think rappelling. One day I hope I can bring some of the girls from my club here. It would certainly be an unforgettable experience for them.

Love, the mountain climber—Donna

❖ ❖

Dear Jesus,

Wow! I love my new apartment—thanks for helping me, Jesus!

My friends, Beatrice and Beverly, are my roommates. We went to Bible College together. They grew up on a farm and they invited me into their home. I had never been to a farm before. Their mom and dad are Christians. They were very kind to me. The dad is really special. I ask him the stuff I wish I could ask my own dad if he was still alive.

The three of us get along well. Sometimes, I hear I don't do the dishes well enough, but that's okay. If they only knew how experienced I really am!

Today I found out I have four impacted wisdom teeth. That doesn't sound good to me. I have to go for surgery and then my face gets to look awful and swollen for awhile.

I met a girl named Rita at the young adults group at my friends' church. She is a lot of fun. We are hanging out quite a bit these days. She is in University studying to be a teacher. She helps me in my club, and so does Beatrice. I am so thankful they are willing to help, and I know the girls really like them.

Rita and I joined a squash club. It is really fun. I would like to tell You I always beat Rita, but sadly I would be lying and You would know that anyway.

Love, Donna

❖ ❖

_____

_____

_____

_____

_____

_____

_____

_____

_____

_____

_____

_____

_____

_____

_____

_____

_____

_____

_____

_____

_____

Chapter 13

Mr. Right

Dear Jesus,

I went out tonight with Beatrice and Rita. We heard different musicians and then a guy got up to speak. He's a garden planter with the Mennonite Central Committee. He spoke, but hardly anyone was listening. I couldn't believe they were so rude! I admit he wasn't the most fascinating speaker, but I could tell he had a beautiful heart.

He worked with First Nations People on a reserve in northern Manitoba. I think he would make a great volunteer at my work, because we work with a lot of First Nations kids. I told Rita I wanted to meet him. I was surprised she knew him. She told me his name is Bill Dyck, and they went to the same Bible school in Europe at the same time.

Well, Jesus, Bill is really nice. When he talks to me, he makes me feel like I'm the most important person in the world. He looks into my eyes when I talk. That is a new experience for me. I don't remember any guy listening so intently. What a neat feeling. I told him about our boy's club, and he said he would check it out. So, I will see him in a couple of days, I guess.

Thanks for a good day, Jesus.

Love, Donna

> *Have you met anyone that you want to thank God for?*

❖ ❖

Dear Jesus,

It has been great to see the girls in my club grow in their faith. They like reading their Bibles and praying now. I told them about going on a ski trip to the mountains. The girls are thrilled. I am too. We will have a great trip. I have to come up with $500 to cover the trip. I will need Your help, Jesus. Please lead me. You always take care of the things I need and I trust You.

Jesus, I am pretty surprised that Bill Dyck phoned me. He can't come to the boy's club, but wondered if I would go to a concert with him. Rita says he is really nice and good looking. His hair is pretty long and wild at the moment, and that goatee isn't my cup of tea. But Rita showed me pictures of Bill without the goatee and I've got to admit—he looks pretty nice under all that hair. So, I guess I will go. I think I can handle his name—it's an improvement over the last guy I knew!

Rita says I might be too wild and crazy for a guy

like Bill, but we'll have to see about that. I am a little tired of men at the moment, as you know. I have found them a bit disappointing. You know what I am talking about. So, Jesus, I am not too sure what to think. I will go. Please come too, okay? Thanks.

Love, Donna

❖ ❖

Dear Jesus,

My 21st birthday is coming up pretty soon. Bill called and asked me if I would be willing to go out to dinner with him. He seems to research all the nicest restaurants in the city and takes me to them. No guy has ever paid me this kind of attention. I told my mom about him. She seemed to be impressed. I met Bill's brother Gerry last week. He seems pretty funny. I also met the girl he kinda dates, Evy. I really like her. She apparently goes to the same church as me. I will have to look for her. She seems like a lot of fun.

I need to go shopping for a dress for this dinner date. I am really not great at this type of thing. I prefer to shop for jeans. It is easier!

I will ask Rita to come. She may be able to help me (not that she wears dresses any more then I do!).

Anyways, a second opinion is always nice.

Gotta go.

Love, Donna

❖ ❖

Dear Jesus,

I am not sure if I am in love or not, but here's the biggest newsflash of the year: BILL DYCK THINKS I'M BEAUTIFUL! No guy has ever said that to me before. Some other good news is that his father is a pig farmer and not a minister. I am glad about that. I told him I was not into boys, I mean, men, at the moment, but I was willing to be his friend. He was good with that. So, we are going skating and for hot chocolate. I should have mentioned I hate skating, but I felt I had been mean enough for one day.

I would be lost without You, Jesus.

Love, Donna

❖ ❖

Dear Jesus,

Thank You for a great day. I am busy trying to raise money for the big trip out west with the girls from my club. Bill came to my office and helped me with the sign. I think every person who works there dreamt up reasons to come and meet Bill. He is cute, though, I have to say. He has big muscles, too. I tried not to stare noticeably. He is very good at making signs. This Saturday, I am going to the mall to sell the crafts we made. I wish they looked better. My mom called. She is going to donate some money toward our trip. Thank You for the neat ways You provide, Jesus.

Love, Donna

❖ ❖

Dear Jesus,

I found out the hard way that it is wise not to try too hard to impress someone. Bill called me and invited me to go to his brother Gerry's graduation banquet. He said his father would be there. Wow, did that put a knot in my stomach. I thought if I could at least have a nice tan that would be helpful. So, I went and roasted in the backyard. The sun was super hot. I thought if I put ice cubes on my eyelids I would stay cooler as I felt like I was burning up.

Well, let me tell you, the ice cubes were a less than brilliant idea. I met Bill's dad and had burnt eyelids. They were even swollen. I was very embarrassed. I don't think he noticed, even though I felt like my eyelids were glowing. Bill thought it was pretty funny. I must say, I will never do that again. Mr. Dyck was very nice. Bill's mom couldn't come because she fell recently and was seriously hurt. She was unable to travel. Bill says that sometimes I remind him of his mom. I think that is a compliment. I hope I get to meet her sometime.

Love, Donna

❖ ❖

Dear Jesus,

I have been thinking lately about what I will do if things don't turn out with Bill. I really like him and would like to see our relationship really grow. He doesn't care about my dad or mom or all the troubles I have lived through. He says it just sounds sad.

One decision I have made I thought You should know. If things don't work out with Bill, I am thinking of becoming a nun and serving in Bolivia. I just don't want to get my heart broken again.

I met Evy tonight at Matt's Place. It is such a neat little restaurant. I like the booths there. The owner knows me now. If you are ever looking for me, that is where my office is. I chose one of the booths there. I like working there better than the office. I seem to get more done. Evy really liked it. She and I ate Smarties and drank a soda.

We solve a lot of problems together. If only the people with the problems would apply our solutions we skillfully dream up for them!

I give You my future, Jesus. I know You have it figured out even if I don't.

Love, Donna

Does it ever seem to you that everything works out for everyone except you?

❖ ❖

Dear Jesus,

I love the girls in my club. My brother Doug came out and visited me. Beatrice and Beverly's parents let me host a "Welcome to the West" party for Doug. We invited the people from the college and careers group at church. We had a really nice cake for Doug. He felt pretty special and celebrated. I was glad he could meet all my friends, and especially Bill. They seemed to get along well. But then I think anyone who doesn't like Bill should go for counseling, as I think he is the nicest person I have ever met.

I am planning on going home for the summer weddings. Vandra is marrying a guy she met in high school. Elly is getting married, too. I am in both weddings; it will be a lot of fun. I am hoping Bill will be able to come to at least Vandy's wedding. That would be neat, and then the people at home could meet him.

Life is changing pretty fast all around me. Soon there will be baby showers instead of weddings. I can't even imagine it.

Thank You, Jesus, that in all the pathways of life, You walk with me. I put my trust in You. I know You are faithful and will never leave me. Thank You for Your constant presence, Jesus.

I love You,

Donna

❖ ❖

Dear Jesus,

It was really neat so see Vandy and Elly get married. I think I have enough long dresses to last me a lifetime. They both picked really nice guys. I was so sorry Bill could not be at either of the weddings. He and Gerry have been working together painting grain elevators. I guess it is a pretty good way to make money. Bill is in his last year at Bible College this year. I wonder what he will do when he graduates?

All my girls' clubs are going great. The girls are all growing in their faith. These girls lead very hard lives. I am so thankful they have You, Jesus, to walk with them every day.

Love, Donna

❖ ❖

Dear Jesus,

Rita and I got an apartment together. We sure have fun. I really need to learn how to cook. If I don't make spaghetti, the only other option is hamburger helper. Rita is better than me at the whole cooking thing. It would help if we owned even one cookbook.

We are having Bill and his friend Ken over for supper tonight. I hope they like spaghetti! I am going to bake peanut butter cookies, too. They are the only cookies I know how to bake. It seems like kind of a weird mixture, but when you are limited in choices, this is the price you have to pay.

When I go home for Christmas, I am going to get Mom to teach me how to bake something else, like chicken!

Thanks for listening to me, Jesus.

Love, Donna

❖ ❖

Dear Jesus,

I am so excited that Bill and I are both flying to Ontario together for Christmas. His family lives about an hour from my mom's apartment. So, he is going to come and meet her and he has asked me to come to his parents' farm and meet his family. I am excited and terrified at the same time. I asked Bill how many girls he has brought home to meet his parents, and he said none. I found a nice gift for Bill for Christmas. I hope he likes it.

It will be great to be home. I look forward to seeing Vandy and Elly. I will find out how they are finding married life. Doug is always good to hang out with. We always have a lot of fun playing games. My mom loves games. I think we all do in my family. I asked Bill how he feels about games, and sadly he is not a games person.

Rita and Beatrice and I are putting together a Christmas party for the girls in our club. We really dream up some pretty crazy things for them. I think they will love it.

Love, Donna

❖ ❖

Dear Jesus,

It was so neat to introduce Bill to my family. My aunts and uncles were even there and met Bill. They all seemed to like him. When they all left, Bill asked if he could give me my Christmas gift. He and Doug disappeared for a while, and then they came out carrying a beautiful, handmade rocking chair. Bill made it for me in his father's shop. Bill said that when he was 16, his parents gave him a lathe. He is really good at it. I have never received such a beautiful gift! My family was super impressed.

The most important thing to tell You, Jesus, is this: When Bill was leaving, he asked me to walk with him to his car. As he was saying goodbye, he told me he loved me! I told him that was very good, because I was pretty sure I loved him, too!!

I am so excited. I don't think I am going to sleep tonight.

Thank You for giving me someone so wonderful who even loves me back!!

Love, Donna

Have you ever been so excited you couldn't sleep?

❖ ❖

Dear Jesus,

Today was a day I will not forget very soon. Bill's family was soooo nice. They laugh a lot. I thought his brothers would be quiet and gentle like Bill. They are not. They are lots of fun, though, and they love to tell stories. He has four brothers and two sisters. Three of his siblings are married. The wives all seem nice. I bet they all play piano and bake and stuff like that! After they told a lot of stories, it was time to sing. I thought they were joking. They brought out the Christmas carol sheets and started to sing! It was like being in a choir. I have NEVER seen a family do that. It was so incredible to just listen to them. I sang but I was pretty overwhelmed. The whole family knows You, Jesus, and loves You and it is incredible to be with them. It is so different from the Christmases I have experienced in all my life.

Bill is like his mom. I don't know how Bill could ever think I remind him of her. She is quiet and a woman who is rich in faith and wisdom. Bill's dad is more on the outgoing side and a really nice man. He works hard. Bill says he is an amazing example of how he wants to live out his faith.

Thank You for a really special Christmas. It has been full of many great experiences that I will never forget.

Love, Donna

❖ ❖

Dear Jesus,

Today, Rita and I went to buy a couch for our living room. We have been living without one for months now. We didn't find a couch, but we did find a really cute kitten. We forgot to mention it to our girlfriend who has been staying with us. The poor girl almost had heart failure when the kitten came running into the kitchen while she was talking on the phone, and climbed up her leg like it was a tree trunk. It would have hurt a lot less if she had been wearing pants. The kitten really is a bit on the wild side. It is at its best when it is sleeping. I found out Bill is not that wild about kittens or cats. I see he will need to change his opinions, because I love them, as You know. I think cats are viewed a little differently when you grow up on a farm.

Please lead me in my relationship with Bill. I think he is the nicest guy a girl could ever dream of. I am a little worried, because we are serious opposites. We both love You and the outdoors and that is about it for similarities... oh, and we both love ministry. That must be worth something.

Love, Donna

Do you have a relationship you could ask Jesus to lead you in? Maybe to give you whatever help or wisdom you need?

❖ ❖

_____

_____

_____

_____

_____

_____

_____

_____

_____

_____

_____

_____

_____

_____

_____

_____

_____

_____

_____

_____

_____

_____

Chapter 14

Let the Bells Ring

Dear Jesus,

Today, Bill and I were out together and he asked me if I would marry him. I would like to say that it was really romantic, but that would be lying. I was thrilled when he asked me. He is very kind and super patient. My mom always said that I would need to marry the most patient man in the world.

He is going to write a letter asking my mom. I know she will say yes. We hope to get married this summer.

I can't wait to tell Rita! She is coming through the door now, so I need to go. Thank You, Jesus, for the amazing gift of Bill Dyck.

I hope I sleep tonight!

Love, Donna

What dreams do you have that you hope and pray with your whole heart will come true?

❖ ❖

Dear Jesus,

I introduced all my girls from the girls' club to Bill. They all seemed to like him. My mom said that she would give her consent to Bill and me getting married. A lady from my home church has offered to put together a wedding for me. We only have a few months to plan.

Please keep Bill safe. There is a little voice inside me saying Bill will die on the way to the wedding. I can't believe something this wonderful would happen to me. Jesus, please walk with me through all this. I can honestly say this is all new to me.

Love, Donna

Do you believe that God has good things planned for you?

❖ ❖

Dear Jesus,

I am having some second thoughts here. I don't know what Bill's family is going to think about having me. I am the second non-Mennonite to join them. That is the good news. Her dad is a minister, though. That must count for something. Then all women in that family seem to cook, sew, garden and, of course, they sing! Lord, I feel so unworthy and unqualified to be a part of this family. How in the world are they going to accept me? I hope they don't ask me what talents

I have. How do I tell them I don't do any of those things? I hope they never ask. I have a lot of learning ahead of me. Bill likes my spaghetti and my peanut butter cookies. He is not hard to impress. That is certainly a bonus!

Love, Donna

P.S. I didn't ask how many of them play the piano. Everyone in Bill's family does! His mom taught them all. What an incredible family.

❖ ❖

_____

_____

_____

_____

_____

_____

_____

_____

_____

_____

_____

_____

_____

_____

_____

_____

_____

_____

_____

_____

_____

_____

_____

_____

_____

_____

_____

_____

_____

_____

Epilogue

How about a cup of tea and warm chocolate chip cookies?!

I would like to invite you to come into my kitchen, sit down, relax, and let me tell you the rest of this story... about a little girl who is finally grown up now.

I love the 40th Psalm, which says in verse 2 and 3: "He lifted me out of a slimy pit, out of the mud and mire he set my feet on a rock and gave me a firm place to stand. He put a new song in my mouth, a hymn of praise to our God."

For me, this Psalm truly represents my experience as a young girl and teenager.

I met Bill and, to be honest with you, my life was never the same after that. He treats me the way I never dreamed I would be treated. He often calls me "his queen," and treats me like a precious jewel. He loves Jesus and serves Him with his whole heart. We have served Jesus in full-time ministry most of our twenty-five years together. We have four beautiful children who love and serve our Lord also.

I recall the countless times I have seen Bill on his knees beside the children's beds, praying for them.

My children think this is normal.

Life is so very different today compared to the valleys I walked so many years ago. The "monsters stored in my closet" have, over the years, still stuck their ugly heads out the door. When they do and all their defeating lies start flying around, I know the truth of what Jesus says and choose to believe Him instead.

Presently, Bill and I and our family minister to the poor and the broken in a church in the heart of Toronto. We have served Jesus in full-time ministry for the last seventeen years. I work right alongside Bill, and we continue to love whoever it is that the Lord brings through the door.

Slowly, but surely, God has brought healing to my heart. While I would not want to walk through the valleys of my childhood again, I am thankful for the journey. The love of my Heavenly Father is my greatest treasure and my faith my most precious gift.

Only God heals the blisters of the soul. He alone can make the valleys bearable through His presence and His love.

Jesus is not afraid of messy lives. He waits for you as He waited for me.

Sincerely,

Donna Lea Dyck

Please visit my website: www.notsoaveragegirl.com. I would love to hear from you! You can email me at: donna@notsoaveragegirl.com. I am also available for speaking engagements.

If you are interested, here are some phone numbers:

Kids' Help Line: 1-800-668-6868

Parents' Help Line: 1-888-603-9100

For wonderful Bible stories you may enjoy:

CEF Tel A Story: 1-877-456-0456

www.wonderzone.com

Winning Kids Website: www.winningkidsinc.ca

 *Not Beyond Our Reach – Book 1* (ISBN# 978-1-77069-359-3), written by Melodie Bissell with Donna Lea Dyck is a companion guide to *Confessions of a Not-So-Average Girl.* You'll find this companion guide highly informative as you reach into the lives of the not-so-average young people in your life and ministry. In it you will find questions that relate to each chapter of *Confessions of a Not-So-Average Girl* to use for discussion purposes.

Not Beyond Our Reach – Book 1 is available wherever fine Christian books are sold as well as through the Winning Kids website listed above, or by contacting Donna Lea Dyck.